THE HIGHLANDER'S PIRATE BRIDE

The Hardy Heroines series, book 7

By Cathy & DD MacRae

PRINT EDITION

PUBLISHED BY
Short Dog Press

www.cathymacraeauthor.com

DEDICATION

To our readers who have
joined us on this
wonderful journey.

Table of Contents

BOOKS IN THE HARDY HEROINES SERIES

Highland Escape **(book 1)**
The Highlander's Viking Bride **(book 2)**
The Highlander's Crusader Bride **(book 3)**
The Highlander's Norse Bride, a Novella **(book 4)**
The Highlander's Welsh Bride **(book 5)**
The Prince's Highland Bride **(book 6)**
The Highlander's Pirate Bride **(book 7)**

The Highlander's Pirate Bride

As the pirate The Black MacNeill, Rona MacNeill has stolen more than one English ship to keep her clan from starving. With Yule only days away, will the theft of the wrong ship land her in a hangman's noose? Or the arms of a Highlander?

Rona MacNeill has done everything she can to help her small, impoverished clan—except marry for money. Her luck seems to lie in stealing ships, not attracting suitors. Only days before Yule, she seeks one last ship with stores to keep her people fed over the long, harsh winter. Too bad her luck has run out.

Pedr MacLean is happy to be the younger (by three minutes) son of Baron MacLean. His days are filled with running the family's shipping business and sailing the world. His heart belongs to the sea—or so he thinks, until one of his ships is stolen, and the woman responsible turns his world upside down.

Drawn to Rona's strength and love of the sea, Pedr will agree to her father's demand—information on the whereabouts of his ship in exchange for his daughter's hand in marriage. Will Rona find herself caught between a marriage of convenience and a hangman's noose? Or will she discover something far more compelling?

The Highlander's Pirate Bride is the swash-buckling seventh addition to the Hardy Heroines series. If you like pirates, rags-to-riches, and swoon-worthy Highlanders, you'll love Cathy & DD MacRae's newest high-seas romance.

WORDS OF INTEREST

Gaelic:

Banríon Laoch - Warrior Queen
cù beag – little dog
Dùdach Mara – Sea Siren
mo leannan - my lover, my sweetheart
mo chridhe - my heart
Nyvaig—little ship (see notes at the end of the book)
Puthaid – Puffin; AKA the *Pèileag* (porpoise)
seoladair – sailor

Scots:

Crabbit – ill-tempered
Gey wheen – a considerable quantity
Pitchkettled – utterly confounded
Skellum – a scamp, rogue, scoundrel

Welsh:

Enaid -- friend; dear one, sweet one; used as a term of endearment.
Wynn – masculine form of 'Wen'; fair one

Norse:

a viking – a term meaning to go raiding
elskan mín – my love, my darling
fífl (FEEF-uhl) — fool, idiot
Megi tröllin taka þig -- translates to "May the trolls take you!"
Skald – a story-teller or bard
Tyr -- A common Viking battle cry — the name of the god of war.

Arabic, Persian, Armenian:

Bari arravot – good morning
Bayt al'asdiqa' – House of Friends
Bayt Alqatat – House of Cats
Be salâmati – cheers or 'to your health'
Marhaba – welcome; the common reply is Marhaban bik (to a man) or Marhaban biki (to a woman)
Sabah al-khayr – a greeting; 'Good morning'; the reply is *Sabah an-noor*

THE HIGHLANDER'S PIRATE BRIDE

Chapter One

Maryport, England
Soloway Firth
Early December 1300

Rona MacNeill crossed herself once then stepped from the dinghy to the stern of the largest merchant ship in port and wedged herself into the gap between the stern and rudder. Heavy fog blocked the night sky and prevented the ship's crew from spotting her approach. The lazy slap of the ocean against the vessel rendered the soft noises she made undetectable. Rona smiled at the gloom, knowing the thick mists created perfect cover.

Her uncle handed her both her daggers and a knotted rope. "Ye sure about this, lass?" His low whisper barely carried to her ears. "'Tis nae too late fer us to find safer prey. In this fog we have our pick amongst these sea birds."

Rona looped the rope over her shoulder, then pulled a black kerchief over her head and face, daggers bare-bladed in each hand.

She patted the ship. "Ye hear the bleating of the sheep as well as I, Uncle. Nae, this fat English lady and her contents shall see our clan through winter. The ship will bring a pretty coin when we sell her to the MacDonnell."

She reached above her head and drove both daggers into either side of the wooden rudder. Using them as handholds to scoot upward, she placed her back to the stern, boots pushing against the rudder. She repeated the movements until she climbed to the top railing, then peered into the darkness for any sign of crew on the aftcastle. A lone sailor lay slumped against the helm, asleep on his watch. Swinging a leg over, she quickly hid in the shadows of the aftcastle railing, waiting for a reaction.

The crewman didn't stir. Rona flipped her dagger in her hand, then drove the pommel into the back of the sailor's head, sending him deeper into unconsciousness.

After tying one end of the knotted rope she'd carried onto a large cleat, she lowered the other end to Oran and her men. She crouched in the darkness and listened for movement, ignoring the cold. Laughter echoed from below as the public women Rona had hired offered their company and cheap whisky to the men guarding the pier. The whisky would warm their bellies and muddle their senses while the women kept their attention diverted this wintry night.

Once Oran and three other of her men stood on deck, she signaled Tomas to return the rowboat to their birlinn. He and the rest of the longboat crew stood by to tow the English ship out to sea. If their errand failed, they were close enough for a cold swim and quick escape.

With Rona in the lead, she and her men descended the ladder from the aftcastle onto the deck, keeping to the shadows. Two more crewmen stood port side toward the dock, likely listening to the women flirt with the guards. She and Broc knocked them out cold, catching the hapless sailors before they dropped into the water and gave away their presence. Carr and Arlen located another *seoladair* asleep at the bow, then slipped silently to a ladder which led below deck to make sure there were no other crew.

Arlen rose from below deck moments later and waved. Carr followed with another unconscious sailor slung over his shoulder. Rona nodded to Broc and Oran, and they released the ropes securing the cog to the dock.

Rona grabbed a rope coiled on the deck with a monkey fist knotted at one end and returned to the aftcastle. Uncoiling a few feet of rope, she twirled the monkey's fist a few times before releasing it to where the rest of her clansmen had positioned their birlinn close to the cog's stern. The knotted ball soared through the mists and landed with a muted thump on the birlinn's deck. She tied her end to the stern cleat. Moments later, Oran joined her at the helm and handed over her fur-lined cloak.

She gave him a reassuring look. "The hard part's done, Uncle. I'll bet my share of the drink below we slip away like ghosties, without anyone hearing anything a'tall."

Oran grinned and shook his head. "I'll nae bet against the Black MacNeill." He jerked his chin toward the prisoners. "What are yer orders for the captured men, lass?"

"Bind them and put 'em in the rowboat once we're away."

Oran descended the ladder to see it done. Rona kept the rudder steady as the ship backed from the dock. The oars of the birlinn worked in tandem with the waves to hide any sound they made. It appeared the holiday revelries had dulled the senses of even the most loyal sailor. She'd chosen the date well.

Once clear of the dock, she tossed the tow line down to Broc who secured it to the bow. Carr, Broc, and Arlen lowered the unconscious sailors into their old tender. They'd awake in a few hours with a headache, but alive. Leaving all hands alive was the Black MacNeill's calling card.

Oran and the others headed below deck to man two of the massive oars, which normally required three men each. Though the fog covered their theft, it also meant no wind for sailing. Rona and her men had a long night ahead, but they only need clear the firth by full daylight. Once they entered the western part of the firth, she knew the north wind would find them.

She pointed the rudder toward the birlinn, allowing the crew to navigate. Huddling deeper into her cloak against the bitter cold, she smiled as she thought of the treasure stored below. The sheep and the price she'd gain from selling the ship were worthy of the risk they all took. Any foodstuffs would pad the clan larder, and all other goods would be sold or bartered for much-needed supplies.

The Black MacNeill they called her. 'Twas a bit of irony as her hair was as bright as the sun and her eyes the clear gray of morning mist. Her coloring and height spoke well of her Norse heritage. Covering her features with black cloth had suggested the name, and it had stuck.

The MacNeill clan was small but proud, claiming the Isle of Gigha as their territory, along with the tiny neighboring islands of Gigalum and Cara. They enjoyed a long history of piracy—one Rona and her cousins happily kept alive. They mostly ignored their Scottish neighbors and instead preyed upon the English, stealing from Longshanks every chance they found. This night's theft was the boldest she'd attempted. They'd gotten away undetected, and with any luck would sail past the Rhins of Galloway before sunrise.

By morning, they'd rounded Cairngaan and the Rhins. As expected, the north wind made a forceful appearance, causing them to tack back and forth as they traveled north by northwest. No longer needing to row, her crew shifted to manning the sail while Rona and Oran took turns piloting the cog.

Oran stretched. "I'll check the cabin and see if they've somethin' to fill our bellies. Keep 'er on a straight course." He clapped her shoulder as he passed. Rona fixed her gaze on the horizon, hoping the sun would bring a bit of warmth.

A sharp bark and a shout of anger yanked her from her musings. She darted to the rail and peered to the deck below. "Anything amiss, Uncle?"

Another bark and low growl parried Oran's reply. "Damned dog! I dinnae know the captain kept a guard in his cabin."

"It doesnae sound verra big. Does he give ye much trouble?"

Oran's rumble didn't quite reach her ears. She laughed.

A few moments later, Oran stumbled up the steps, pausing to shake a leg. He gained the aftcastle, a wee dog attached to his boot. It growled and tugged, clearly intent on inflicting damage.

Rona's chuckles increased. "Och, Uncle, he's scarcely bigger than a large rat. Do ye think he'll get any bigger?"

"Nae if I have anything to say about it," Oran grumbled. "Get by, dog." He jerked his boot from the dog's jaws. Panting heavily, the wire-haired imp stared at its prey before shifting his attention to the two interlopers on his ship.

He set up a frenzy of barking, high-pitched yips that undoubtedly would have carried far over the water were it not for the thick, enshrouding fog.

"Hush!" Rona hissed as she reached for the dog. Quicker than a striking goose, it leapt away, leaving Rona with naught but a tuft of hair and a scrape of sharp teeth.

"Damn!" She shook her hand, eyes narrowing on the creature which had just lost its status as cute.

It cocked its head, but ceased barking, tongue lolling out one side of its mouth.

"Cheeky little bastard, isn't he?" Oran sat on a barrel and opened a bit of linen he'd folded around some hardtack which he shared with Rona.

"Lass, have ye noted the name of the ship, yet?"

Rona nodded thanks as she accepted the biscuit, breaking off a piece which she tossed to the little terrier. "Likely named after some comely wench."

She stole a glance his way. One side of Oran's mouth pulled in and upward as he often did when worried.

"Nae a comely wench, then. Mayhap a flower?"

Oran shook his head. "Nae."

The dog sniffed the hardtack then licked it cautiously, a

skeptical gleam in its eyes as it watched its new benefactor with suspicion.

Rona laughed. “Ye wee skunner. I’ll name ye Murdo for the terrible sea warrior ye are.”

Oran cleared his throat.

Rona shifted her attention back to her uncle. “What has ye puckered up like an auld woman?”

“We’ve stolen the *Puthaid*.”

“The *Puthaid*?” She tossed the dog another bite. This time he snatched it up eagerly and wagged his stumpy tail for more. “Nae Englishman would name his ship the *Puffin*.”

Oran rubbed his whiskers. “He wouldnae,” he agreed. “Makes ye wonder whose ship ’tis.”

Rona shrugged. “Nae matter. ’Tis ours now.”

“Aye. But fer how long?”

Rona grinned. “Until the MacDonnell shows us good coin for her. He can deal with any problems after that. She’ll nae longer be our worry.”

Oran dipped his head but didn’t appear happy.

Two days later, Rona strode into the main hall of the MacNeill keep in Ardminish village, Oran and Murdo in her wake. Her da huddled in his chair before the large fireplace, a blanket over his legs. He glanced up and a smile lit his face.

“Och, the Black MacNeill and her henchman return.” He gestured to chairs near the hearth. “Come. Sit. Tell me the tale of yer adventures. It appears ye’ve added one to yer crew.”

Rona and Oran each took a seat near the fire. Murdo trotted about the room, nose to the floor as he explored.

“A terrier. A keep can never have too many ratters. His name is Murdo.” She rubbed her thumb over the scraped bit of skin on her hand. “He bites.”

“Of course he does.” Laird Galen MacNeill eyed the dog

warily then waved to a kitchen lad.

"Are ye hungry or thirsty, mayhap?"

Rona nodded. "We ate afore leaving the ship, but a couple of mugs of hot cider wouldnae go amiss."

Young Hamish grinned then bolted to the kitchen. Rona waited to give her account until the lad returned. All the lads on Gigha cut their teeth on such stories. She knew the details of their trip would be soon told several times over as a score of clansmen had met them earlier to relieve the *Puthaid* of her burdens. Rona wondered how exaggerated the tales would be by the time the men arrived at the keep for the evening meal.

Hamish returned, red-faced and out of breath, with a pitcher and two empty mugs. Oran shot her a smirk then took the items from the lad and set them on the small table beside them. The boy sat on the floor, a whistle on his lips, a bit of meat in his hand. Murdo cocked his head then quickly approached the lad, accepting both a pat and the treat.

Others in the hall also gathered for the story-telling. Murdo adroitly avoided further pats and slipped beneath Rona's chair where he settled, his gaze on the crowd.

Rona poured a mug for Oran and herself before topping off her da's. She then settled in to hear of Black MacNeill's latest exploits. Oran was the clan's best *skald*, and the crowd was soon enthralled with his tale. She chuckled with his attempt to paint her as a ruthless pirate. What kind of pirate cuts no bloody swathe, and ensures the guards are treated as kindly as possible? This was only his second telling—she heard the first as they unloaded the stolen cog. By this evening, his third account would be even more dramatic.

Once Oran wound down, people went back to their chores and the preparations for the evening meal, smiles aplenty on excited faces. Laird Galen handed his mug over for a refilling. "Is she beached at the northwest bay?"

Rona nodded. "Aye. None shall see her unless we wish

them to." The northwest bay was a narrow inlet with craggy rocks on either side blocking the view unless someone sailed near the mouth. The deep water bay suddenly ended in a sandy beach, making it the perfect spot to hide ships. From there, off-loaded goods were hauled by wagon to the keep and outlying crofts.

"What'd she bring?"

"The cog is on the smallish side, but held fifty ewes, casks of wine and mead, barrels of dried fish, oats, and a few furs. There were also two large jars of some sort of sweet, thick jam. I dinnae recognize the taste. We gave them to Cook to see what he could make of it. I expect ye'll see it on yer table in the morn."

Her da grinned at the mention of sweets, but he quickly sobered. "Though I heard Oran's tale, I wonder if we should expect trouble?"

Oran paused before he answered, then shook his head. "Nae, Laird. The Black MacNeill paid two, er, ladies to ply the guards with whisky. They dinnae hear us board the ship and the crew never saw who laid them out."

"And, yet ye seem uncertain," Galen replied.

Rona chimed in. "Yer brother fears we've stolen a Scotman's ship rather than an English one."

Galen cocked an eyebrow. "And why would he fear that, daughter?"

Rona shrugged. "She's named the *Puthaid*, nae an English name."

"Ye dinnae think to take another ship?"

"'Twas dark with a fog thick as porridge. I dinnae know the name until halfway across the firth."

Galen shook his head and pointed a gnarled finger at her. "Ye should have been more careful. We cannae afford to anger a powerful clan."

For the first time, fear fluttered in her belly.

Oran scratched his beard. "I'll see to it she's renamed.

Arlen's kin by marriage live on Islay. I'll send him to Aonghus Og to barter a price and have her off our hands afore Yuletide."

Galen nodded. "Aye. 'Tis a good plan." His gaze leveled on Rona. "Heed my words, daughter. Ye are responsible should any trouble come our way o'er this."

She was tempted to deny any ill would appear. Hadn't Oran just claimed the Black MacNeill always got away cleanly? Laughter silenced on her lips.

When did she start believing in her uncle's tall tales?

She'd see to it her clan profited from their raid without bringing trouble to their shores. Somehow.

She rose and considered what must be done to rid themselves of the *Puthaid.* She considered setting it adrift but knew her da would never agree to such a waste. With the Holy Days upon them, she hoped the MacDonnell was in a generous mood.

Galen took a sip from his cup. "We'll use the coin from the sale of the ship for yer dowry."

Chapter Two

Her da's pronouncement sapped the strength from Rona's legs and she collapsed back into her chair. Murdo whined.

"What?"

"Ye heard me, lass. 'Tis time ye married. Ye cannae play at being a pirate yer whole life. One of these days, even the Black MacNeill's good fortune will run out."

Rona tried to form a response, but nary a thought surfaced that would not offend her sire.

Galen leaned an elbow on his chair and regarded her with a pensive look. "I've heard from Laird Hamilton of Arran. He's in need of a wife tae raise his weans."

Rona rallied with a snort. "I'd be his fourth wife I know of. He's an auld man, Da. Some of his children are older than me. He doesnae need a wife. He needs a minder."

Galen gave a thoughtful nod. "Aye, he's got a few summers on me. What of Laird MacDougall of Loch Ryan? His eldest son, Boyd, is a braw laddie."

"Da, Boyd may one day make a fine leader and husband, but he's still a wean. He's better suited as a playmate for Murdo than a husband for me."

Her da narrowed his eyes. "Ye'd have a hand in his raisin'. Help shape him into the kind of husband ye want."

Rona groaned and buried her face in her hands, striving to regain her composure. She knew better than to raise her voice. Da would pick the worst of the offers just to spite her for arguing.

He sniffed. "I dinnae ken how many years I have left. Once yer Uncle Oran is chief and starts a family of his own, what then?"

Rona considered his words. Accommodations in their old keep were limited. She'd need to move out of the laird's family chambers on the top floor. And go where?

"I'd likely find a croft near the ocean and help with the ships."

Laird MacNeill curled his lip. "Help how? The clan allows ye aboard the ships 'cause ye're my daughter. Dinnae expect the same indulgences once I'm buried."

Rona's good intentions fled at his dismissal of her efforts. "Those *indulgences* brought fifty sheep, food to help see us through the winter, and plenty of dry goods for trade."

Her da leaned forward, eyes ablaze at her response. "Aye, and mayhap a powerful clan to our doorstep. I'll ask about tae see if there might be other offers, but heed my words. Ye'll marry afore spring. If ye dinnae make a choice, one shall be made fer ye. I want that cog sold and gone afore the new year."

Rona stood and stiffened her spine. "Aye, m'laird. 'Twill be done as ye say."

* * *

MacLean Castle
Morvern
Loch Aline

Pedr and Alex sat across the desk from the Baron of Morvern—their laird and da—Birk MacLean. Pedr glanced at his twin, hoping he had insight as to why they'd been summoned. Alex's miniscule shrug told him he was as much in the dark as Pedr.

He tilted his head in their da's direction, telling Alex, as the eldest and therefore the MacLean heir, it was *his* duty to address their da. Alex frowned then cleared his throat.

Baron MacLean did not let him speak. “We await yer ma.”

Pedr’s mind searched for what matter might require both their parents in such a formal setting and came up with nothing good. He couldn’t recall any trouble he or Alex had created recently, nor any their cousin Brant—learning to captain his own ship one day—had assisted in. ’Twas doubly ominous Brant hadn’t been summoned to his da’s solar as well.

He sighed. It would serve no purpose to question their sire further and would only provoke the bear.

His need to break the tension grew. “Do ye wish me to send for refreshments?”

His da scowled at the question, then nodded. “Aye. Yer ma would appreciate mulled wine and mayhap a small plate of sweets.”

Pedr launched from his seat and bolted for the door. Anything to escape the rising pressure in the room.

“Return immediately,” the baron barked.

“Aye, Da.”

Pedr took his time, bypassing two servants he could have charged with the task. Brant MacCain stepped from the shadows of a pillar, worry lining his brow. He’d inherited the MacLean clan’s dark eyes, but his reddish blond hair was proof of his da’s strong Norse heritage. Nearly the same age as Alex and Pedr by less than a month’s time, his easy-going, often mischievous nature and love of the sea marked him more like Pedr than Alex.

“Have ye learned anything?” Brant asked.

Pedr shook his head. “Nae. We await Ma, but I’ve been sent for refreshments.” He glanced about. “’Tis a good enough reason to leave Alex to handle Da for the nonce.”

Brant nodded. “Aye. If anyone can reason with him, Alex can.” He shrugged. “I think I’ll take myself off to the docks. The *Dùdach Mara* is coming along nicely and should put to sea for the next trading season." His face softened as he spoke of the MacLean's newest merchant ship.

Pedr cuffed his shoulder. "Hoping to be tapped as her captain, aye?"

Brant's cheeks colored. "I'd relish the chance," he avowed. "I've sailed the passage to Lebanon once with ye and saw things I'd ne'er dreamed of."

"The MacLeans once laid claim to a large portion of land there. My great-greatgrandma was an Armenian princess."

"What happened? Ma told some stories, and I've heard a few more since I've been here."

"When my great-greatgranda returned to Scotland, he left men to run the castle and help set up his shipping business. My grandda still held the title of Baron of Batroun, and he visited often.But nae long after he and my grandma Hanna wed, the entire Crusader state of Lebanon fell to the Mongols and Mseilha Castle was razed."

"Have ye seen the site?"

"Och, nae much left to see. Romans built the first fort there, so the foundation's fairly solid. A few bits of wall here and there." Pedr drew a breath, remembering the awe he felt to stand where his ancestors had once lived and fought. "I'll take ye there one day. Donal MacLean is yer great-greatgranda, too."

"I'd like that. I'm verra glad to join MacLean Shipping. I'd be happy to be named first mate until I have a few more years at sea and can earn my own ship."

"Ye may get the chance," Pedr replied, once again glum. "Whatever Alex and I've been summoned for, it doesnae seem likely Da is handing *us* his latest ship."

Brant sent him a sympathetic look then hurried from the hall. Pedr watched with envy as his cousin gained the freedom of the bailey, then continued with his errand.

He lingered in the kitchen, drawing out the chore as he

waited on his ma. He was no longer a lad needing to hide behind his ma's skirts, but neither did he need to stew under the force of his da's glower. He'd likely say something foolish to try and ease the mood. Da rarely appreciated his humor. Neither he nor Alex shared their da's fierce personality. They both leaned more toward their ma's calm manner.

Pedr spotted his ma's wavy, dark hair and confident gait as she came down the stairs, and waited for her, arm extended. She smiled and grasped his elbow.

"Ah, my chivalrous son. Do not think I will give away yer father's intentions for this meeting simply because ye play the gentleman."

Pedr struck his chest with his fist. "I am wounded my lady mother would think me so underhanded. Did I nae recently swear to treat all ladies with great respect upon earning my spurs?"

Carys cocked a brow. "Mayhap 'tis years of watching ye use yer charm on unsuspecting females—from yer nurse as a wean to, more recently, the village lasses—that makes me wary."

Pedr plastered a smile on his face to hide his embarrassment at her astute observation. He opened the door to the chamber and bowed, allowing his ma to enter first.

Baron MacLean and Alex rose.

Carys glanced at the men and shook her head. "'Tis like living amongst giants. My sons may share my dark hair and eyes, but they tower above me as does my husband. Even young Brant has the MacLean height."

"Aunt Gillian is shorter than ye," Pedr noted as he followed his ma inside the room.

Carys patted his cheek fondly. "Aye, she is."

The men sat once she chose her seat. A gentle knock on the door announced a serving lad with a tray of refreshments, another lad with a pitcher and mugs.

Carys inclined her head. "Thank ye both."

The lads poured and distributed the drinks before departing.

Pedr shot Alex a glance to determine if he'd learned more. Alex pursed his lips in the negative.

Birk smiled. "Lads, yer ma and I have discussed yer futures. Ye've both done well this past year, Pedr with the shipping business, and Alex helping me run the clan. 'Tis time for the next step."

Carys leaned forward. "What yer da is trying to say, is we've invited a number of families from neighboring clans who have daughters of marrying age to join us for the high holidays. Neither of us had much say in our first marriages . . . ."

She cut a glance to her husband. Both Alex and Pedr knew the story. She'd had almost no say in her second marriage to their da, though it had worked out famously. Who didn't like a ma who could guide her family and clan with a gentle yet firm hand—and best their da in sword play if he needed a reminder to not push her too far?

The hesitation passed. "We'd like to offer ye the ability to choose. The Holy Days provide an opportunity to host visitors and strengthen alliances."

Pedr shifted uneasily in his chair and considered how to avoid his da's ire. "I understand why ye wish Alex to marry and ensure the line, but why me?"

Birk's eyes narrowed. Carys forestalled his response with a raised hand.

"Ye both have a score of summers. 'Tis time to think about raising yer own families. The two of ye have ever been inseparable. Yer da and I thought 'twould be easier if ye focused on the task at the same time."

Pedr glanced at his sire. The restrained storm his ma kept at bay lay ready to erupt should he or Alex offer anything but an aye. Resigned to their fate, Pedr slumped forward, elbows on his knees, and nodded.

A scratch at the door interrupted and Birk shifted his glare. "Come."

The dockmaster entered and touched his forelock. "Beggin' yer pardon, m'laird, m'lady, young sirs. 'Tis rather urgent."

Birk waved him forward. The man strode to the desk then bowed and handed Birk a slate.

Birk's face reddened as he scanned the writing on its surface. "Someone stole the *Puthaid*? My—ship? My *newest* ship?"

The dockmaster winced then nodded. "Aye, m'laird. The cap'n and crew just arrived this morn from Maryport. Someone subdued the crew on watch then slipped away in the night."

"No one saw a thing?"

"Nae, m'laird. Cap'n says 'twas as foggy a night as he's e'er seen."

Carys rose then walked to the desk and picked up the message. "How many dead?"

The dockmaster scratched his head. "Weel, now, 'tis an odd thing, m'lady. Mayhap a blessing. The five left aboard were found the next morn trussed up in a rowboat floating near the shore. All complained of headaches and a few bumps and bruises, but none were seriously harmed. The cap'n is pitch-kettled."

"Sounds like the Black MacNeill," Alex offered.

The Black MacNeill was rumored to leave those he stole from humiliated but alive. Strange conduct for a pirate. He was surely more legend than fact.

The dockmaster shrugged. "Mayhap, young sir, but all ken the Black MacNeill only preys on English ships."

Pedr jumped at the opportunity to be away from Morvern this Yuletide. "She was in an English port. Mayhap he mistook her as English. Da, why dinnae I talk with the captain and crew, then see to the search? Whoever the thief, we cannae let this insult pass."

His da and ma shared a glance. Birk waved a hand. "Aye. Take Haldor and yer uncle Sten with ye. They've known Captain Shaw as long as he's sailed for us, and any likely places a stole ship might be found." His lips scrunched to one side, clearly struggling with a decision.

Carys raised a brow at Birk's choice of assistance. The unspoken message was that their Uncle Sten and his son Haldor had been pirates before Pedr and Alex were born. They'd know better than any what questions to ask—and mayhap the best way to return a stolen ship.

Birk continued. "Take young Brant as well. He needs time aboard ship. Haldor is home for the winter, and I dinnae believe Sten, as the MacLean shipmaster, will appreciate pirates spiriting away a ship he's just completed—especially on her maiden voyage."

Pedr nodded, hopeful he'd found a way to escape the marital noose tightening around his neck.

His da pointed a thick finger his way. "Dinnae think to get out of the evening entertainments. Ye shall both be presentable for company each evening at supper."

Pedr and Alex sighed. "Aye, Da."

* * *

A sennight later

"If I have tae sit through another discussion about the latest court gossip, I may leap from the north tower." Pedr slipped his nicest leine over his head.

Alex, already dressed for supper, handed him his plaide. "Och, who knew there were so many hen-brained lasses in Scotland?"

"Aye," Pedr replied, much aggrieved. "Nae one of them

can sail, shoot a bow, or wield a sword like our ma or Ama."

Alex laughed. "Do ye seek a bed partner or sparring partner?"

Pedr grinned. "Why not both? Da has both, as did grandda Alex if the stories about Ama Hanna are to be believed."

Alex nodded. "She may be an auld woman, but Ama is plenty fierce. We MacLeans do have a reputation for strong women. Aunt Gillian is nae pampered lily."

Brant snorted. "Nae one would call my ma pampered."

Alex pointed to his cousin. "See? He agrees." He turned his attention to Brant. "Ye're happy because ye are a cousin—and a youngest son at that—and happy to nae be facing marriage."

Brant lifted a mug of ale. "Nae. Ma'll nae think of me any time soon. I've two older brothers and a sister already wed and giving her bairns to care for." He grinned. "'Tis good to be a child my parents never expected."

Alex laughed. "Nae. Yer sister was surprise enough, coming twelve years after they thought to be finished with bairns. Ye, a year later, was enough to cause Aunt Gillian and Uncle James to wonder if they'd figured out where bairns come from."

"So, ye've chosen Peigi Stewart," Pedr noted, drawing Alex's ire.

"What's wrong with Peigi?" Alex demanded.

Pedr spread his hands wide. "Dinnae mistake me. She's a sweet lass and fair to look upon."

"And brings a firm alliance," Brant added.

Alex smiled broadly, humor restored. "Aye, and she possesses a wicked sense of humor."

Pedr glanced at his twin in surprise. "Truth?"

"She isnae likely to take up arms to defend the keep like Ma, but she's enjoyable company. We're both happy with the match."

Pedr patted Alex's shoulder. "I'm greatly pleased for ye, brother." He forced a smile to cover his dismay. He knew he'd never settle for a woman who could not match the strengths of his ma and ama. But where to find a lass who loved the seas and a fight who didn't have the temperament and appearance of a swineherd?

Alex playfully punched Pedr's arm. "We've plenty of men at arms. If I need to depend on my wife to defend hearth and home, we're likely already lost. Dinnae fash. Ye may find a good woman tonight."

"Are ye an eejit? They mostly ignore me because I'm nae the heir."

Alex shrugged. "Once Peigi and I announce our betrothal this eve, ye'll be the only MacLean son nae taken. I know we're used to Da's rich holdings since we grew up here, but for most, Morvern is a palace."

Pedr groaned and shook his head. "Aye. 'Tis worse. All the lasses who wish for finery will now point their gazes my way." He peered at his cousin. "Mayhap they'd consider Brant a good mate."

"I'll admit, there have been a fair few who seem to have a wee bit of greed in their eyes." Alex joined Pedr's needling. "We can certainly boast of his merits. He cleans up well and has the broad shoulders the lasses seem to enjoy."

Brant bolted upright in his chair. "There's nae need for that! I'll marry when I'm ready—and it won't be for some time. I'll watch as the lasses vie for yer attention, and happy to remain in the shadows."

"Och, aye," Pedr tossed at him. "Alesta MacDunn muttered under her breath between bites during supper last week. I believe she was keeping a running appraisal of all she saw. 'Tis nae a stretch to say, Avarice, thy name is Alesta MacDunn."

Alex barked a laugh. "Is that what she was on about? I figured the thought of marriage to either of us had her reciting her rosary prayers."

Brant rubbed his chin. "What about Ghleana MacCraig? She's nae a small, wilting thing. She'd give ye big, braw sons. A bit on the quiet side, but that's nae a bad quality in a woman."

"Aye, she's quiet, all right. Dinnae ye understand why?"

Brant shook his head.

"The lass is feeble-minded. I'm nae saying she's completely daft, but how do ye carry on a conversation with a woman who cannae string together more than a few simple words?"

Brant chuckled. "Hmm. I see. Ghleana isnae a good choice for ye. Come on, cousin. They arenae all bad. What about Oona MacBrea? She's a winsome lass."

"She's quite bonnie, but each time I asked her a question after the evening meal, she made a face like she'd eaten something foul. I suspect she either had a bit of wind from supper, or she's *crabbit*."

Pedr sighed and ran a hand through his hair. "Alex is the heir. I dinnae need to marry a lass to satisfy da."

Alex tossed his brother his belt. "How goes the search for the *Puthaid*?"

Pedr brightened at the change of subject. "Hard to say. We've offered a reward for any information and spread it across our captains and allies. We talked to Captain Shaw and crew, but they saw and heard nae a thing. The first mate said he spotted the dock guards cavorting with a couple of, er, ladies, that night. The way he says it, they all shared a jug or two."

Brant smirked. "Drunk and distracted. That's clever."

"Aye. Too damned clever. Have ye heard tell of any pirates to be so careful and nae leave bodies?"

Brant shook his head. "Nae. I was skeptical at first, but I think ye may be right to suspect the Black MacNeill."

Pedr tightened his belt then slipped a small jeweled

dagger in the sheath at his waist. "The only problem is, nae one knows who he is."

Alex cocked his head. "Someone knows. Likely someone in the MacNeill clan. Ye might start there."

Chapter Three

Twin Harbors
Isle of Gigha

Rona paced the sand, eyes on the letters gracing the bow of the ship. Murdo raced down the beach, barking ferociously as seagulls fled before him. “The paint looks good, Uncle, but the shape of her aftcastle and mast are unmistakable. ’Tis still the *Puthaid*.”

Oran grinned. “Nae, lass. Ye can read better than that. ’Tis the *Pèileag*.”

She shrugged. “I like the name. Porpoises are sleek, and the *Pèileag* is verra seaworthy.” She touched her thumb and forefinger to her chin. “Do ye think we can convince the MacDonnell to buy her?”

Oran spread his hands wide. “We shall pray he does and doesnae question her origins. Arlen and I will leave in the morn and travel to Loch Indaal and see if Aonghus Og is in residence.”

“I pray ye safe travels, Uncle.”

“Och, dinnae fash, Rona. He will receive us, we will trade well for the ship, and we’ll be home in Ardminish before the Yule log is lit.” He thumped her shoulder. “Dinnae fash over yer da. Ye brought enough goods to give our clan a right hearty holiday.”

She rolled her eyes. “Da is fit to be tied because she’s a Scottish ship, nae English. The sooner she’s out of our hands, the better. I dinnae wish to bring trouble to Ardminish Bay.”

“’Tis a gift ye brought the clan, niece. Food and sheep to

carry us through the winter. We stand to make a nice sum on the sale of the ship which should see us into the spring."

Rona squared her jaw. *I swear we willnae use the profit as my dowry.*

* * *

Aboard the Banrion Laoch
At sea, between the Isle of Jura and the Kintyre Peninsula

The brisk wind whipped Pedr's cloak, its chill fingers brushing his cheeks. His position at the bow invited the wind's caress, as compelling as that of a lover. He was at his best aboard a MacLean ship, even one his cousin captained rather than the *Puthaid* which lay beyond his reach for now.

His entire family owed their wealth to the merchant line his great-grandsire had established more than eighty years earlier as well as the significant treasure Donal MacLean had brought back after years of successful trade in the Levant. The thought of giving up life on the sea for a wife he had little care for disturbed Pedr greatly and he let slip a mild curse at his parents' meddling which could cost him much of his freedom.

Today, however, he would hunt a pirate.

He resisted the urge to rub his hands together in anticipation.

Footsteps approached on the deck.

"'Tis the Isle of Gigha just ahead." Brant nodded toward the land on the horizon.

"We'll sail east past the northern tip and should put into Ardminish harbor within the hour," a second voice added.

Pedr inhaled deeply. "Thank ye, Captain Haldor. I'm looking forward to this."

Haldor chuckled. "Ye've more than a bit of piracy in yer heart, young Pedr. 'Tis a good thing yer da has raised ye to the conscientious life of a merchant. Ye'd be a right fierce adversary if 'twere otherwise."

He tapped Brant's shoulder. "This one is true to his Norse family. His love of the sea cannae be denied. I'm certain 'twould nae take much to lead him *a viking*."

Pedr grinned, reminded he had more than a little Norse blood himself. "A bit of larceny doesnae generally appeal, but chasing down the gallows bird who stole the *Puthaid* gives me a sense of . . .."

He squinted into the gathering dark clouds, hunting for the correct word.

"Of *righteous indignation*?" Haldor laughed. "Ye'd make a fine pirate were ye nae so honest." He clapped Pedr's shoulder. "Look lively. We're comin' into the harbor soon. Da wanted to know if ye wish him to speak with Laird MacNeill, or if ye would?"

"Uncle Sten may be of an age with the MacNeill, but I'll handle this." Pedr couldn't stem the excitement racing through him. "Och, I'll handle this."

Dogs barked at Pedr's heels as he strode from Ardminish harbor toward the MacNeill Keep. A light drizzle descended, causing Pedr to tug his hood over his head. Broc MacNeill, the man who'd greeted them at the dock—albeit with surly reluctance—led Pedr, Sten, and two silent guards inland. More MacNeills trooped at their heels, faces stern and unwelcoming.

"Ye'd think they dinnae see our rail bristling with soldiers and arms, the way they attempt to intimidate us with their glower," Pedr remarked in a low voice to his uncle.

Sten—some ten years older than Pedr's father, and a pirate, once, himself—shook his grizzled head. "Our show of arms was what kept them from turning us away. And may be all which allows us to return to our ship. We've stepped into a den of pirates, laddie. Dinnae think we hold the upper hand now that we're beyond the reach of our ship. We're now at their mercy, and I'd rather walk out alive than be assured our men will avenge us."

Pedr sobered. A battle would be costly in lives and he did not wish his men or himself to be counted among the dead.

They continued in silence except for the slosh of a worsening drizzle until they at last reached the keep.

"I'll ask ye to leave yer weapons here." Broc MacNeill's hard gaze stilled the retort on Pedr's lips.

Sten shook his head. "We will swear to nae draw a weapon save in defense of our lives, but we willnae strip ourselves of our swords."

Broc conferred with one of the other men.

"Wait here." Broc's curt command left the MacLeans clustered beneath the dubious shelter at the doors, exchanging glowers with the MacNeills as the drizzle slowly turned to sleet.

Pedr drew an oatcake from his sporran and amused himself by tossing bits of it to a pair of sea gulls braving the weather to argue over the treat.

A few minutes later, Broc returned. The glint in his eyes told Pedr the man did not like what his laird had to say.

"Follow me."

"A man of few words," Pedr remarked, feeling like a pup baiting a wolf. And from the looks of things, a hungry wolf.

Only a handful of holiday greenery graced the mantle above the hearth. Most of the light in the room came from the fireplace and two slender openings high in the wall, though a pair of candelabra—tallow candles smoking in the draft—sat upon the head table next to a wooden pitcher and a tray of bannocks. A worn fishing net, bits of shell and sparkling stone tucked among its tattered lines, hung above the fireplace, and someone had tucked a few sprigs of ivy among the strands. A man with a great shock of white hair sat in a chair by the hearth, a heavy blanket draped over his legs.

His eyes glinted in the dim light. His lips did not curve in welcome.

"Come. Sit by the fire and warm yerselves."

His words did not convey friendliness.

Pedr stepped to the hearth. "My thanks for yer hospitality, Laird MacNeill. I am Pedr MacLean, here on behalf of my father, Baron MacLean." He gestured to Sten. "My uncle, Sten of Hällstein."

Laird MacNeill's eyes flickered at the mention of Sten.

Och, so pirates do *have long memories. Uncle Sten gave up pirating long years ago—when my ma married my sire. Fascinating how his reputation lingers.*

The MacNeill grunted. "Broc tells me ye seek a ship. I've nane to sell."

Pedr allowed a small smile. "I'm nae buying. I seek one which was stolen a sennight ago."

"And ye think to find it here?"

"Och, nae. I wouldnae think ye'd keep such a thing lying around." Pedr glanced about the chamber. "And I saw naught in yer harbor resembling the ship we lost." He fixed his gaze on the laird. "But this isle has many harbors. And 'tis rumored the Black MacNeill is again sailing the seas."

"And ye think *I* could be the legendary pirate?" The laird grimaced. "'Tis well-known the shipwreck which cost my wife her life nearly claimed my legs as well." He spread his hands to indicate the blanket over his lap. "I havenae walked without pain in nearly a score of years. The deck of a ship is beyond me." His eyes narrowed. "I assure ye, I'm nae the Black MacNeill."

Pedr returned his steady gaze. "Mayhap ye could tell me who is."

Wind whipped the door to the hall open, slamming it against the wall. Water splattered on the floor as a black-clad figure raced inside.

"Da! There's a strange ship . . .."

The young woman skidded to a halt on the stone floor. Her gaze slewed from the laird to Pedr and Sten.

"My apologies. I dinnae know we expected guests."

Her hair, dark with rain and sleet, lay plastered against her head, one heavy strand straying across her forehead. Her cloak, made of supple, well-tanned seal hide, dripped water onto the floor. Boots showed beneath the hem which rode several inches above her toes.

Smoky gray eyes stared intently at Pedr. He grinned.

"Good evening, my lady. I am Pedr MacLean."

Her eyes widened and she cast another look at her da.

"My daughter, Rona. My only child," Laird MacNeill said. He leaned back in his chair and sent Pedr a speculative look. "Baron MacLean's son, ye say? Ye've a twin."

Pedr startled. This had nothing to do with his lost ship or pirates. The hairs on the back of his neck rose in warning.

"Aye. My brother Alex. I run the shipping business."

A wily grin lit the laird's face. "Ye run the shipping, eh? Could that mean yer brother is yer da's heir? I heard a rumor there have been quite a few lassies paraded through Morvern this past sennight. Lookin' fer a bride, is he?"

"Da." Rona's voice rumbled in warning.

Pedr's brows arched. A tremor darted through him, and his heart skipped a beat. How did he go from hunter to hunted?

He firmly quashed the urge to run.

"He has chosen a bride," he managed, his voice steadier than he'd feared. "The betrothal was announced yester eve."

Laird MacNeill fingered his whiskery chin. "What about ye? Have ye taken a bride?"

Pedr shot a panicked look to Sten. His uncle shrugged.

"I'm here seeking a ship, nae a bride."

"Of course ye are, laddie."

Laird MacNeill motioned to a serving boy hovering at the doorway. "Pour our guests some hot ale and ask Cook to provide a tray. We mustn't stint on hospitality, and supper is an hour away."

The lad scurried from the chamber. Pedr glanced about the room, noting again the barrenness of the hall. There would likely be no feast at the MacNeill keep this holiday season.

At the MacNeill's gesture, Pedr and his men settled into chairs. Rona slipped the cloak from her shoulders and draped it on a hook near the hearth. Her slim figure displayed admirably in leggings and tunic. She appeared nothing like the lasses taking up space at the MacLean tables this week past.

Her hair, beginning to dry about her face, had lightened, and shimmered gold in the firelight. Pedr rather liked the effect.

The old man set his gaze on his daughter. "Rona, these gentlemen are here about a ship. Ye wouldnae know aught of a ship which shouldnae be in our harbor, aye?"

The look she shot him pricked Pedr's curiosity.

"We've naught but our own birlinns, Da."

Laird MacNeill nodded slowly. "Young Pedr MacLean asked about the Black MacNeill. Would ye know aught of the pirate?"

Her eyes widened, then she scowled. "The Black MacNeill is naught but a legend. A story to scare weans who misbehave."

Pedr leaned forward, forearms on his knees. "The legend is of a pirate who doesnae leave a wake of blood and death. What sort of pirate leaves crewmen and guards alive—albeit with a lump on their heids as big as a ploughman's fist."

"As I said, a legend," Rona retorted. She turned to the

laird. "Da, if ye'll excuse me, I wish to change out of my wet clothes."

Without waiting for his consent, she bolted for the stairs.

Laird MacNeill waved a hand. "Forgive my daughter. She's nae in the first blush of youth and having a man such as yerself in the hall has addled her wits."

Again, the hairs on the back of Pedr's neck spiked. "Do ye have something ye wish to say?" he demanded.

A smile spread on the laird's face. "I have a proposition for ye. In return for information about yer ship, I'll ask ye tae wed my daughter."

The serving lad appeared and placed his tray on the low table next to the laird. Distributing mugs of steaming ale, he bowed then departed at a sharp look from the MacNeill.

Pedr sipped the ale, his mind addled with the import of the chief's offer.

Brant would never let me hear the end of this. Not for the first time, he reaffirmed his decision to leave his cousin aboard the *Banríon Laoch*—against his protests, to be sure. But Pedr needed him to help carry word back to Morvern should things go awry at the MacNeill keep—and not pester him about bids of matrimony from Laird MacNeill.

He sighed as the ale's warmth spread through his belly, grateful for the interruption which allowed him a moment to think. "I doubt ye have enough information to warrant marrying yer daughter."

Laird MacNeill slathered a nearly translucent golden spread atop a thick slice of bread and handed it to Pedr. He accepted the offering and opened his mouth then paused, the bread halfway to his mouth. The aroma of sweet oranges wafted to his nose. He cut his gaze to the laird who stared at him, an eyebrow quirked upward, a small challenging smile on his lips.

The *Puthaid* had been carrying marmalade.

Chapter Four

Rona's boots shushed over the stone steps as she hurried up the stairs, their worn soles soft and supple.

Thanks be to Saint Oda for getting Oran out of the twin beaches before the MacLean's emissary arrived! She'd not expected him. No, that wasn't true. She'd considered the possibility but hadn't wished to believe it would actually happen. Of all the clans to steal from—the MacLeans would not have been her choice.

Nor had she expected to nearly lose her wits at the sight of Pedr MacLean's sardonic grin.

What was wrong with her? Had her da's talk of marriage done something inexplicable to her? Addled her previously competent wits? She neither wanted nor needed the distraction of a husband. She was quite content to play the part of the Black MacNeill and tend the needs of her clan. A tall, dark-haired Highlander with the easy stance of a sea captain would not change her plans.

So, why did the memory of his smile plague her?

Rona jerked the door to her room, swearing loudly as the wood, swollen by the damp weather, grated stubbornly against the floor. Another tug drew it reluctantly open, though its groan of protest could likely be heard on the mainland.

She put her shoulder to the panel and pushed it firmly closed. At least she always had expectation of warning should anyone attempt to breach the ancient bit of wood. Ha! As if she had aught to steal.

She shivered despite her agitated mood as she stripped out of her damp garments and ran a rough bit of linen over her skin to dry the lingering moisture. Pulling a heavy wool blanket over her shoulders, she huddled before the hearth. A clack of nails on the bare wooden floor told her Murdo had slipped from the bed.

"Leaving yer comfortable berth to greet me?" The thought cheered her and she ventured a quick scratch atop his head. His low grumble of warning was spoiled by the jerk of his stubby tail.

"All bark, eh, laddie?" She rubbed beneath his ears. Murdo showed her his teeth but pushed against her when she ceased petting him.

"Ye dinnae know who to trust, do ye? Ye dinnae like being taken from yer ship, but I promise things will go well for ye. We've plenty of rats for ye to dispose of, and ye willnae be mistreated. Young Hamish has a soft spot for ye, if I'm nae mistaken." She grinned as he tilted his head, white, spiky fur sticking out in all directions around his face, pointed ears catching her words.

"I like ye, as well."

The faint embers in the fireplace did little to heat the chamber, but peat was precious and she decided to add only a single block to encourage a bit of warmth. Smoke rose, filling the chamber with an earthy perfume, bringing a welcome calm.

What did Pedr MacLean know? None besides her closest clan members knew of the ship which had sat at harbor until only this morn, and only she and her crew knew the ship's name. None on Gigha would betray the Black MacNeill.

It wasn't likely Pedr MacLean was doing more than fishing for information. If he knew she'd stolen the *Puthaid*, he certainly wouldn't have smiled at her. She heaved a disgruntled sigh.

Where had he gotten the impression the Black MacNeill had stolen his ship? Och, she'd left the crew alive—the calling card of the legendary pirate. Bad time for that bit of goodwill to come back to haunt her.

Warmed, she rose and discarded her blanket. Murdo sniffed about the room as she dressed. In an attempt to give nothing away as to her secret—mostly secret—identity, Rona set aside her usual leggings and tunic, choosing instead a demur gray wool gown, its original dark blue color only revealed at the seams where washing hadn't scrubbed the dye away. She yanked a comb through her hair and tied it with a bit of ribbon from the small, carved casket which had belonged to her ma.

Until Pedr MacLean and his men were away from Ardminish, the Black MacNeill would remain a legend.

The hall was empty of the MacLean sailors when Rona returned, Murdo tagging at her heels with a growl to one of the keep's cats which stepped too close. His jaunty step kept him nearly beneath her feet. She almost tripped over him twice, but he would not be parted from her side.

Her da glanced up from his seat near the hearth, and though it would have been an easy task to avoid him, she could not with good conscience flee the room. Again. Though she desperately desired to. She dreaded the coming conversation more than a tooth pulling.

His stormy mein grew darker than the clouds fouling the sky as she approached. The sleet whistling outside had naught on the cold glint in his eyes.

"What did I tell ye?" he hissed. "Nae good would come of stealing a Scotsman's ship! *Sell it to the MacDonnall*, ye said. *'Twill be nae problem*, ye said." He collapsed against the back of his chair and glared at her through bushy brows. "Ye've brought the MacLean's son with more men than we can defend against to our door with yer recklessness."

"My *recklessness* is all that 'twill keep us this side of starvation this winter," she reminded him. Murdo whimpered unhappily and Rona tempered her frustration.

She nodded to the empty room. "It appears he exited the door just as quickly as he came."

Galen snorted, his mood softening. "He and his men will be staying the night."

She whirled on him. "What?"

"I've struck a bargain with young Pedr."

Her eyes narrowed. "Da. What have ye done?"

His gaze cut to the low table beside his chair. Rona stared at the clutter of mugs and bannocks and . . . *marmalade.*

"Ye served him his own marmalade? What were ye thinking?" Rona's heart tripled its beat, yet the blood seemed to drain from her head. The edges of her vision darkened and she gripped the back of a chair for support. Murdo pressed against her leg. "He'll know the *Puthaid* was here."

"Just so. I warned ye, lass, and now 'tis time to pay the price fer yer foolishness. Ye've played at being a pirate long enough."

"Ye've been quick enough to reap the rewards of my *foolishness*," she growled.

"Be that as it may, I'm settling my affairs." Her da's chin jutted forward, his eyes glinted, daring her to argue.

"Settling yer affairs? Ye expect to shake hands with Auld Boneshanks soon?"

His chin lifted a notch and his gaze slipped away, but he did not reply.

"Da, Uncle Oran will make a fine laird when ye finally seek yer rest, but ye're an obstinate auld bastard and likely to outlive the rest of us."

"I doubt that." He glanced down, picking at the blanket across his lap. Rona noted the whiteness around his lips and the lines furrowing his brow. Did pain or stubbornness cause his grimace?

He met her eyes. "I have a hankerin' fer a bairn to

doodle on me knee." His chin rose again. "I'd know my grandchildren before I die. Ye are my only daughter and 'tis time ye acted like it."

Fury rose. Her hands fisted. "So ye'd sell me to a man who will leave me home to birth his bairns whilst he plays at the only thing I've ever loved? Trapped in a life of runny noses and fouled cloths when I've lived with the swell of the sea beneath my feet and fresh sea air in my lungs?"

Hurt sliced through her anger. Tears pricked the backs of her eyes. She would not agree to this marriage, no matter what he'd promised Pedr MacLean.

She knelt beside his chair, placing her fingers atop his gnarled hand. "Da, I dinnae wish to marry. I dinnae *need* to marry. My heart belongs to the sea and to our people. Dinnae go through with this. I willnae agree to wed him."

"I wish tae leave this world with ye wed and a roof over yer head. Marriage to Pedr MacLean will give ye much more than that."

She shook her head. "I cannae live a life imprisoned on land. Dinnae ask it of me."

Her da glanced over her shoulder, his jaw set. "'Tis too late. Negotiations have already begun."

She rose. "Well, ye can just halt the negotiations. Ye should have asked me first. 'Tis yer own fault if he cries foul."

"Och, he willnae cry foul. And ye *will* wed him."

Her hands fisted on her hips to hide their tremble. "Why is that?"

"I've promised him information to find his ship."

Pedr glanced about his chamber. There was no fire on the hearth, and a rime of ice sealed the wooden shutter closed over the narrow window slit. He huddled deeper into his fur-lined cloak.

"Nae much of a welcome," Sten noted with a wry glance

around the poorly-appointed room.

"I regret any family lives as such," Pedr replied, his quiet tone offering sorrow for the MacNeill circumstances. "Had I known, I might have given them the damn ship. At least the contents," he amended. He ran a fingertip over the ice on the shutter.

"I'm surprised ye accepted Laird MacNeill's offer to stay the night." Sten narrowed his eyes. "Ye arenae seriously considering marrying his daughter, are ye?"

Pedr turned from the window, his head at a thoughtful tilt. "There's something about her. Something compelling."

"Ye found wet hair and trousers compelling?" His uncle laughed. "Ye could have yer pick of the lasses in yer family's hall this past sennight."

"Lasses with an eye for my family's wealth or my brother's standing in the clan. Nae for me." Pedr waved his hand as if banishing the proffered potential brides from his sight.

Sten snorted. "This one'd do well to wed ye. Are yer pockets deep enough to bear the brunt of supporting yer relatives by marriage?"

Pedr's lips pulled to one side. "I couldnae leave them to starve. Something'd have tae be done. Da isnae going to like supporting the clan that stole his ship."

Sten chuckled. "Yer da may regret insisting ye wed. This could tweak his nose out of shape a fair bit."

Pedr grinned. "'Twould serve him right for forcing the matter. He and Ma wish me to choose the woman who pleases me."

His uncle raised an eyebrow. "And this lass pleases ye? Why?"

"Good question, Uncle. I cannae say for certain, except, she reminds me of someone."

"Nae much to recommend marriage, Pedr. Mayhap an evening in her presence will help."

Pedr nodded. "That, my uncle, is why we are staying."

"I thought ye stayed to wring a confession from the MacNeill—without tying yerself to his daughter."

Pedr grunted. "Regardless, I want the information promised to find the ship. 'Twould put me in Da's good graces to return home before Yule with the *Puthaid*."

"The MacNeill laird had quite a reputation in years past. Dinnae let him get the better of ye. It wouldnae surprise me if *he* carried the name of Black MacNeill when he was younger."

"Do ye believe Laird MacNeill stole the *Puthaid*?"

"Nae. Ye saw him. 'Tisnae possible he had a hand in the actual theft. My guess is there's someone close to him, a brother or nephew, mayhap, who executed the deed, though the laird may have planned it. If they're smart, the ship is long gone from here."

"Where?"

"They have an alliance with the MacDonnell," Sten said, his voice dropping an octave on the last two words. Clan MacLean certainly did not align with the MacDonnell. Quite the opposite.

Pedr nodded. "Aye. 'Tis true. Rumor is the MacDonnell has a fleet of ships—nae all Scottish built."

A sardonic grin spread over Sten's face. "I'd be willing tae bet they're English."

Chapter Five

Pedr and Sten rejoined the others in the hall. Their MacLean guards had been offered space in the crowded chamber with some of the MacNeill clan to sleep that night, but instead, would take up places in the passageway before the small room on the upper floor which had hastily been cleared to accommodate Pedr and Sten. Guests of the MacNeills they might be, but it didn't serve to be lax in their guard.

People filled the hall, taking the benches closest to the hearth first, the late-comers left to claim seats on the chilly side of the room. A heaping platter of broiled fish sat on the head table, and all helped themselves fillets of cod and pollack, and a chunk of bread. Serving lads walked the tables, filling mugs from steaming pitchers of cider.

Open hostility as well as furtive glances greeted Pedr and Sten. Voices dropped to mutters and whispers. Laird MacNeill waved them to seats next to him.

"Come. Sit. Me daughter will see tae yer supper."

Pedr scanned the room but did not see Rona MacNeill. Disappointment slid through him. There was something about her . . ..

A young woman in a faded blue gown, her bright hair secured by a faded ribbon, settled a platter before each of them, then waved to a serving lad. A wee white terrier padded at her heels, avoiding the crush of feet around him. Pedr sat in the chair indicated, then glanced up. Cool gray eyes met his. He startled. Did the MacNeill have two daughters?

Nae. He claimed only the one. Pedr stared in disbelief.

This could not be the same woman who'd stormed into the hall earlier, bringing icy winds and a no-nonsense attitude.

But it was. Though her hair had dried and now shone like gold in the firelight, and she'd exchanged her tunic for a simple gown with tight fitted sleeves and a worn surcoat of coarse wool, the high cheek bones and defiant scrutiny marked her as Rona MacNeill.

She pursed her lips and averted her eyes.

So, the lass plays at being demure. I wonder why?

He quelled a grin as his interest grew. Her gaze darted back to meet his and for an instant, he thought fear flickered in her lovely eyes.

Laird MacNeill's words echoed. *I want ye to marry my daughter*.

Had there been no suitors for the lovely MacNeill lass? Even in the worn gown, she was a striking woman. Her height would put her near his shoulder. She moved with a grace that captivated him, a rolling stride which suggested she'd spent time at sea. She appeared an age to be wed and with a bairn or two on her hip. Was she widowed?

Could Rona hold an objection to marriage? He peered at her, noting the fine lines at the corners of her eyes. The pale band of skin at the line of her hair, though her cheeks and nose were rosy enough.

She must spend time outdoors, he decided as he settled back in his chair. A good thing to note, as there were plenty of tasks to running a household which required outdoor activity. She likely was adept at gardening, and possibly even lent a hand fishing in the shallows, catching bait-fish for the men. No wilting flower, this Rona MacNeill.

Something stirred inside, tugged at his heart. It must be difficult tending her clan with so few resources. The urge to care for her startled him. Was he truly ready to give up much of his freedom and take a wife? His da's demand that he be wed battered his futile desire for freedom. Surprisingly, the resentment toward the notion of marriage had vanished. The reason for his change of heart stood across the hall, supervising the feeding of her clan.

Pedr studied her again, though she'd turned her back and appeared to instruct a lad on serving ale. Her gown stretched tight against the width of her shoulders, and the hem cleared the floor by nearly a hand's breadth. Did not the laird's daughter merit a new gown?

The thought he could dress her in lush velvets and shimmering brocades brought a smile to his lips. He would see to it she had all the finery a woman could want. When he came home from his travels, he'd bring her sparkling trinkets sure to please her. Aye, she'd be a fine wife to return home to after months at sea. Thoughts of fleshly pleasures filled his mind.

Sten jostled his arm. "What has ye lookin' like a fox what just ate a fine cockerel?"

Pedr blinked. Lady Rona was gone. He craned his neck searching for her, but to no avail.

He shrugged. "Counting my chickens before they hatch, nae doubt."

"Still thinkin' of marrying the lass?" Sten shook his head. "I never thought I'd live tae see the day. Keep to the sea, laddie. Ye dinnae need the distraction of a wife."

"Da expects me to return with his ship before Yule. We've but a few days left."

"He wants ye wed, as well," Sten pointed out. "Though it might take longer to find the *Puthaid* without MacNeill's help, do ye wish to marry a woman ye dinnae know?"

"I'm reserving judgement," Pedr protested, anxious to keep his uncle's good opinion. "And I know her as well as any of the lasses Ma and Da have paraded through the castle hall this past sennight. Rona MacNeill's the only one who merits a second look. Ye need a year or more to truly know someone. Did ye know yer wife when ye married, Uncle?"

Sten rubbed his grizzled beard. “Aye. Ye’ve a fair point. Ye’re a ship’s captain, Pedr. ’Tis in yer blood. Haldor and I were once pirates, and though we’ve mended our ways, we’ll always tread the planks. The sea’s a demanding mistress, lad. ’Twill take an uncommon woman to pull ye from her clutches.”

“Ye think to warn me from the lass?”

“Nae. But will she understand yer love of ships and far-off places?”

“She’s seen plenty of ships in and out of Ardminish Harbor. ’Twill be naught new for her. Of all the lasses I’ve met, Rona is most likely to understand my time away.”

He propped the end of his eating knife on the table, handle in his fist. “In fact, the more I think on it, the better I believe Rona MacNeill fits my needs in a wife. She’s sturdy, bonnie enough, and doesnae fear work.”

Sten snorted. “I have a horse that fits those requirements, laddie. *I* wouldnae marry ye if *I* was yon lass. I cannae think of a woman alive who appreciates being called sturdy—or being told they’re *bonnie enough*.”

Pedr frowned. Mayhap those weren’t the best points to make. “After living her life in this hall, she’ll be grateful nae to have to worry about her next meal. Da will agree to assist the MacNeills in some fashion if they become family.”

Sten nodded. “Aye. Any lass ye bring home will likely be grateful for what yer family offers.”

Pedr nodded, though uncertainty wrestled with anticipation. Something about her called to him, and he wouldn’t leave the isle until he’d learned more about her.

He turned his attention to the meal, careful to eat only enough to take the edge off his hunger, mindful this was likely a larger offering than customary. There was plenty of food left aboard ship, and it would do him no harm to avoid stuffing himself this night when it was clear others needed the food more.

"Have ye eaten enough, young Pedr?" Laird MacNeill pointed to the platter of fish at the head table which boasted a single fillet remaining in a thin puddle of a congealing buttery sauce.

Pedr patted his stomach. "Plenty, my lord. Filled all the necessary corners."

"Excellent. Let the lads clear the tables and we'll get back tae our business." He peered about the room. "Where's me daughter?"

Rona stepped through a small crowd of departing clans people. Servants and those who would shelter in the hall overnight had retreated to the kitchen or the far reaches of the room.

"I'm here, Da." Her skin quivered, alert as a hare beneath the intense scrutiny of a hungry fox. What did her da have in mind?

Laird MacNeill's eyes glittered for a moment before shifting to Pedr. "Have ye considered my offer?"

The large, white-haired man next to Pedr crossed his arms over his chest. Clearly he and Pedr did not agree, whatever the answer. But, who agreed to her da's offer and who did not?

Pedr angled a bit sideways in his chair and propped an elbow on the table. "Aye, I have."

Her da raised his eyebrows. "Are ye willin' tae marry me daughter for information on yer ship?"

Pedr's gaze slipped to her. Speculation warred with pity in his dark eyes. She liked neither. She liked even less the feel of a cattle auction and would have stormed from the room had the stakes not been so high.

"Before ye hunt for parchment and ink for a betrothal contract, I'd like to know—since we already agree my ship isnae in yer harbor—how ye will help me. I say 'tis the work of the Black MacNeill, yet ye claim he's but a legend."

Her da raised a shoulder, his lips curving down. "Legends are peculiar things."

"Pirates have their place—though 'tis often enough on the dangling end of a knotted rope. Do ye mean to tell me ye harbor a pirate?"

Rona's blood pounded in her ears and the air whooshed from her lungs. She grabbed the back of a chair to steady herself. Would he see her hang? 'Twas within his right.

"I mean to tell ye I can help ye find yer ship," Galen replied stubbornly. "But ye'll have to agree to my terms."

Pedr's gaze cut to her. Her defiance wobbled.

Look elsewhere for yer ship, MacLean. Dinnae cast yer luck with me.

"Give me yer information." Pedr's tone was implacable. "I will wed yer daughter if yer information helps me recover the *Puthaid*—within the week."

Galen slapped the tabletop. Rona flinched. Murdo yelped and burrowed beneath the hem of her gown.

"Done! Rona, tell the lad where his ship is."

Rage boiled in her veins and she scowled. "I dinnae know where 'tis."

"Come, lass. Ye sent her off this morn. Tell young Pedr where she's headed."

Rona crossed her arms over her chest and gritted her teeth. How could he do this to her?

Pedr glanced from Rona to Galen. "How would she know of the ship? Do ye think to deceive me?"

Galen waved a hand. "Och, dinnae fash, young MacLean. This lassie knows verra well where yer ship is." His lip curled. "Did ye nae steal the *Puthaid* from the harbor at Maryport three days past?"

Rona sucked in a shocked breath.

"And did ye nae see that she was renamed so ye could sell her?"

Rona leaned over the table, hands fisted on the scarred

wood, face only inches from her da's. "Aye. And I put sheep in yer pens and food on yer table," she spat. "And for that, ye'd see me hang?"

"I'd see ye wed. I said ye'd take responsibility if ye brought trouble to our shores."

Pedr's eyebrows rose. "What are ye telling me, Laird MacNeill?"

Galen pointed a gnarled at her. "I'm tellin' ye, me daughter is the Black MacNeill."

Chapter Six

Pedr shook his head then blinked his eyes. He couldn't have heard Laird MacNeill right. There was no possibility *she* . . .. He drew back and marshalled his thoughts. Why not? The woman who'd blown into the room earlier, stormy-eyed and dressed in black, lent credence to Laird MacNeill's claim, though he'd think twice before crossing the woman who faced him now—especially if she had steel in hand. The possibility piqued his interest. A wife adept at wielding a blade? Yet another point in her favor.

Defiance drew her to her full height, but fear sparked in her eyes like lightning amid roiling thunderheads. Did she think he'd demand she hang for her crime? *Crimes*? How many stolen ships could they lay at her feet? English ships until now, if the stories were to be believed. Saint Andrew's crooked toes! Had he agreed to wed a pirate? Bollocks! Not merely a pirate, but the notorious Black MacNeill!

Sten nudged him then gave a nod to the little terrier. "'Tis a MacLean ratter."

Pedr followed his uncle's gaze and stared at the little dog, scarcely making the transfer from believing Rona a pirate to the wiry-haired pup which bore the unmistakable stamp of the white terriers his ma had bred for the past ten years or more. Many people now owned the loveable imps, but their main purpose was as ratters aboard all MacLean ships.

Even on her maiden voyage, the *Puthaid* had a MacLean terrier.

By the wart on Saint Andrew's nose, if Rona wasn't the Black MacNeill, she knew who was.

Pedr rose. "I believe 'tis time to take this conversation to a more private place. Laird?"

Laird MacNeill frowned then waved a lad near. "Prepare the hearth in my solar."

The lad darted off. The terrier bounded forward, yipping encouragement.

Rona pivoted on her heel and stalked in the lad's wake, anger holding her shoulders rigid and quickening her stride. The wee dog trotted jauntily alongside, his stubby tail pointed toward the ceiling. Pedr stepped from the table and strolled after Rona, leaving the others to follow.

He reached her as she stormed into a small, cold room lit only by the protest of a tiny flame on the hearth. The lad crouched next to it, blowing gently as he coaxed the flickering fire to life with bits of lint and dry twigs. He cut his gaze from Lady Rona to Pedr, then ducked his head, making himself as small as possible as he sought a quick exit.

"Is what Laird MacNeill said true?" Pedr demanded. He grabbed the door and swung it closed on the people who approached the room. It wasn't likely such a secret—if true—would surprise the MacNeills, but he was determined to hear the words from Rona's mouth, untainted by her father's ire or the need to temper her response.

Rona halted then slowly turned. Her eyes the color and intensity of a winter storm met his. "If it was?"

Saint Andrew's fire! Pedr eyed her with admiration. *I could search from the Minch to the Mediterranean and not find another woman like her.* His gaze moved from the stubborn tilt of her head, down the curve of her neck—lingering on the swell of her breasts which would fit the palms of his hands quite nicely—and to the fists clenched at her side.

He lifted a brow. "'Twould brand ye as a pirate, and, as such, subject to the laws of Scotland."

Her face paled, bright spots of color in her cheeks. "That would be unfortunate, as it would render Da's offer invalid. Unless ye prefer the title of widower to husband."

An oft-told tale—usually resulting in his ma's delight at his da's displeasure and embarrassment—came to mind. *Yer da asked me to consider if marriage to him was better than a hangman's noose. I told him 'twas a difficult decision.*

Pedr ground his molars to defeat the grin rising to his lips. His da had been guilty of forcing his ma to wed to avoid the hangman's noose when she was arrested for poaching MacLean deer. Some argued the claim was unfair, though her da had considered the ploy expedient at the time. After a somewhat rocky beginning, no one would deny his parents had an unshakeable bond. Dire circumstances had forced them to work together, bringing each a great appreciation for the other. What would be better than to uphold such a family tradition?

His ma would likely skelp him were she to discover his ploy. He would take pains to ensure that did not happen, but it tweaked his sense of irony, nonetheless. He risked her further ire by wedding Rona on the isle without family other than Sten and Haldor and Brant in attendance. A formal ceremony could later be held at Morvern which would satisfy his ma's and ama's need for welcoming his new bride into the clan.

The mischief-making side of his nature rose, and he couldn't resist. "'Twould prove quite a difficulty to be a widower at such a young age. Howbeit, ye may rest assured the power of my family would keep ye safe."

Her eyes widened. "Ye would ask me to exchange a hangman's noose for a marriage I dinnae want?"

This time the grin would not be denied. "Lass, I've twenty summers, am in good health, belong to a family of fairly substantial wealth and influence, and—if ye were to ask about—considered rather amiable, moderately fair of looks, and generous with those I have dealings with. Ye could do far worse than marry me. If yer sire is willing to corner his own daughter into marrying into a clan of means using the threat of a hangman, who are we to cry nae?"

He could have sworn steam escaped her ears. Certainly, she seemed to be without words for a few moments. Someone pounded on the door. The terrier startled.

"Do I have nae choice?" Rona's voice was brittle.

Pedr strove mightily for a morsel of sympathy—or at least regret—but 'twas no use. For whatever reason, her disinclination to wed only made him want her that much more.

"I fear ye dinnae. Yer da appears quite committed to this alliance. Once we are wed, ye will fall under my protection, and none will gainsay me. I would certainly nae bring charges against my own wife for theft of a MacLean ship." He glanced about the tiny room, gaze lingering on the shabby furnishings as he shivered in the cold which was due to the clan's need to heat only rooms under use. "And I wouldnae see my wife's family in need. Ardminish makes a fine port and we've always needs for experienced hands who wish tae earn coin aboard our merchant ships."

Rona's chest heaved. Her hands curled, longing to grip a blade. She did not know where she wanted to bury it more—into her sire's black heart, or into the man standing before her. She'd never been so livid in her life. Angry, dismayed, perhaps even anguished—but not even Carr's pranks as a lad had driven her to such extremes. Revenge, aye, but not to the heights of outrage and the sense of betrayal her da and Pedr MacLean induced.

She jammed her fists into either hip. "I am certain—were I to ask—ye could supply references to yer temperament, assiduousness—and mayhap even the condition of yer teeth. But the fact remains, I dinnae wish to wed."

Pedr paused and cocked his head as if considering her words. "If ye lived the rest of yer life to yer choosing, what would the years look like?"

Rona hooked a foot around the chair at the desk and dragged it close before plopping into it, arms crossed, as if she'd suddenly deflated. Murdo abandoned his snuffling in the corners and settled next to her, his wee head resting on her feet. No one had cared what she wanted before. Would Pedr's interest prove different?

Her hands folded in her lap. "I only wish to serve my clan."

"Becoming a pirate was yer best plan?"

She scowled. Insolent man. "Born with a gold coin clenched in yer fist doesnae make ye the best person to make choices for me. The MacNeills may be poor, but we are self-sufficient for nearly all our needs, one way or another. Besides, Longshanks and his toadies deserve what I've done—and more—for their evil deeds against our countrymen."

Pedr nodded. "I cannae find fault with the Black MacNeill's revenge against the English. Ye're a braw lass for taking up arms against such an enemy."

Rona stared at him. Was he proud of her accomplishments as a pirate?

She remained speechless for a moment before sweeping an arm to one side. "Look about our island. We've nae enough fertile land on this rock to keep the clan fed. I'm the laird's daughter. What sort of woman would I be if I dinnae do all I could so my people wouldnae suffer?"

"Sheep and a bit of marmalade make a nice Yuletide gift," Pedr noted with a slight smile.

She shot him a bold look. "Aye. They do. We also will have fine wool to keep bairns warm next winter once the sheep are sheared this spring. Mayhap a bit of meat to add tae the table which has been limited tae fish." She rose, suddenly strengthened by the good she'd done by stealing the *Puthaid* and those ships before it.

"Wine and mead for drinking and for barter. Oats which we cannae grow enough of on this isle. Dried fish to supplement our winter stores." She faced him. "And the coin we get for the ship will go a long way in trade in the spring."

Pedr nodded. "A fair accounting. Ye clearly know of the *Puthaid.* I confess to being hard-pressed to see ye as the pirate, the Black MacNeill, but I at least believe ye had a hand in the ship's disappearance."

A faint smile of mockery lit her lips. "Ye dinnae believe a woman can be a pirate?"

Pedr appeared surprised. "Nae. I'm quite clear a woman can be whatever she wishes. My great aunt successfully defended a castle in the Holy Land. My ama knew the sorrows of the Scottish battle for the Western Isles—and swore revenge against the Scots, though, fortunately for me, fell in love with my grandsire. My ma fought against Longshanks during the Welsh wars for independence, and, on her voyage to Scotland, routed pirates more than once."

Something in her shifted. Could it be the fact his family had no more love for King Edward than she? Or that Pedr MacLean seemed different from the men she knew who had little regard for a woman except when she was on her back or providing other comfort?

How far could she trust this MacLean's honor?

Another knock pounded the door. Unintelligible words rumbled through the wood.

She considered the man before her. Taller than almost any man she knew, dark brown hair nigh as black as his eyes. Eyes which held challenge, a glimmer of kindness—and humor. What kind of man offered marriage to the pirate who stole his ship rather than exact revenge? Would such a man prove a worthy husband?

"Ye believe I stole yer ship?"

He shrugged. "Och, aye. 'Tis clear ye did."

"Clear? How?"

Pedr grinned and nodded at the terrier sitting at her feet, eyes peering through wiry tufts of white fur. "Yer pup. Each of our ships has at least one of Ma's terriers on it to keep the rats at bay. Nae only did ye steal the *Puthaid*, but ye stole the ship's wee dog as well."

Chapter Seven

Well. She hadn't expected the dog to give her away. Rona stared at the little white terrier. His stubby tail beat a tattoo against her leg. She bent and scratched behind his ears then glanced at Pedr. "Will the captain want him back?" A pang of regret shot through her at the thought of losing the wee scamp.

He shrugged. "I wouldnae worry about it. The pup appears to have taken to ye. Captain Shaw will be pleased to know he's come to nae harm."

A single thud on the heavy portal announced their time in private was coming to an end.

Rona heaved a reluctant sigh. "Shall we open the door?"

Pedr shook his head. "Nae until we reach an accord. I would have ye sign yer name willingly to the contract. A reluctant or rebellious wife isnae my intention."

Rona chewed her lip. Whether she was ready to wed or nae, she wasn't likely to receive a better offer. A different pang tugged at her heart. She'd been so busy protecting her clan, she'd given no thought to what her heart would desire. Could marriage with Pedr MacLean be more than a clan alliance—and a way to avoid the noose? Was she foolish to wish for more?

"Even were I nae facing a hangman's noose, my options would be between ye and the next male who is of an age to sign his name," she pointed out. "Da willnae relent."

Pedr spread his hands wide. "I'm nae such a bad catch, Rona. I care for my own and dinnae abuse women nor children." His eyes twinkled. "And I'm still in possession of all of my teeth. I could show ye if ye like."

A laugh bubbled unexpectedly in Rona's throat. Why not wed the MacLean's youngest son? No matter what she did, her days of striding the planks appeared over. An hour ago, the admission had embittered her toward men of all ages—especially those who claimed to only have her best interests at heart. Now? The scoundrel appealed.

"Mayhap marriage to ye would be preferable to the hangman's noose," she allowed, fighting the beginnings of a smile.

"Spoken like a woman who knows her own mind," Pedr declared. "Pragmatic and insightful. Shall we seal the bargain with a kiss?"

Her smile vanished. Entering into a contract with Pedr was one thing. Allowing intimacies was another. Yet, there was no separating the two. Marriages formed alliances. Alliances grew dynasties. Children were required to inherit those dynasties.

She reined in her thoughts before they became full panic. He asked for a kiss, not a tupping on her da's desk. Inhaling a slow breath, she composed herself and gave a nod.

"Preparing for battle, eh?" Pedr shook his head. "I'll nae storm yer decks, cutlass in hand. I'll nae be that sort of husband. Ye have my word. I've a different sort of wooing in mind."

An exhilaration not unlike facing a storm at the bow of a ship rushed over her. She swallowed, throat suddenly dry. "This isnae going to be a peck on the cheek, then?"

His grin was pure seduction. "Nae, lass. I dinnae have pecks in mind." He reached a hand toward her. "The first step is yers."

"Och, thank God. For I dinnae know what the second step is."

She took his hand and did not resist as he drew her before him. The room, boasting little more than a sullen glow of peat on the hearth, was suddenly much too warm, the walls much too close, her gown—albeit one she'd outgrown months earlier—much too tight.

Pedr closed the final distance, his cheek nesting against the top of her head. "Promise ye'll always fight for those less fortunate than ye," he murmured, his breath stirring her hair. "Promise ye will always tell me what ye think."

A strangled chuckle escaped her. "Ye have naught to fear. I dinnae dissemble well. And, my heart will always be with those in need."

"Yer sympathies, aye." He pressed his lips to her hair, the corner of her eye, the ridge of her cheek. "Yer heart, my fair pirate, belongs to me."

Rona swayed but held firm. It would do no good to hold him responsible for her predicament—though he didn't have to look so pleased. She'd given her best endeavors to her duties as the Black MacNeill, she would not quail at giving like attention to her responsibilities as Pedr MacLean's wife.

She would allow one kiss.

She awaited the rough plunder she'd witnessed from sailors and the women who met them at the ports. Pedr did not oblige.

His hands skimmed her shoulders in a languid fashion, setting up tingles that buzzed through her veins like the first swallow of a sparkling mead. His lips drifted lower to linger on the corner of her mouth. At his touch her face turned.

His lips brushed hers, soft, warm, inviting. A breath of anticipation separated them, hot, tantalizing, seductive. The tip of his tongue outlined her lips. A faint gasp fled Rona's throat. Pedr deepened the kiss, then, when her world tilted firmly beyond her control, drew back. Her lips followed, pulling her up on her toes, hands splayed on his chest, fingers fouling the cloth of his tunic.

His arms swept about her and pulled her tight, his body rock-hard against hers. She pressed closer. A moment later, he lifted his head.

Pedr cupped her face in his palms. "Open the door, my pirate lass, and I'll pen the appropriate words for our betrothal."

Pedr forced a smile and silently encouraged her to turn away—anything to give him time to compose himself. He'd meant to kiss her. Meant to test her resolve—and his. He hadn't meant for the kiss to light fires he had great difficulty subduing. But he didn't like the uncertainty which flared in her eyes. Was there an enticement he could offer? Something that would persuade her to look forward to returning home with him?

"If ye've nae objections, we will speak our vows on the morrow and celebrate at Morvern once we've recovered the *Puthaid.*"

Her face whitened, eyes flashing. "Of course. The ship comes first." She whirled about and was at the door in two long strides. She wrenched the latch and flung open the portal.

"Rona," Pedr protested. *Damn. Could I have worded that worse?*

She ignored him.

"The wedding is set for tomorrow," she informed the pack at the door. "Do whatever ye deem necessary." She shoved past her da who blustered at the impropriety of lingering behind closed doors with a man not her kin.

Rona halted long enough to favor her parent with a scowl. "Challenge him if ye think ye can best him. But, dinnae kill him. 'Tis my prerogative, now."

Sten, Laird MacNeill, and two guards who assisted the laird to his chair, parted as Rona stormed through their midst and was gone. Pedr scratched his head.

"Well, shite."

"I've nae seen a lass flee ye before," Sten needled, sounding much like Alex and Brant in that moment. "Nor with plans for yer demise." He rubbed his chin, eyeing his nephew. "Have we called off the wedding?"

"Things were going well until I mentioned the *Puthaid*. Innocently, I swear." Pedr raised a hand against his uncle's chuckle. "'Twas well-meant, and I only said we'd wed here and celebrate at Morvern." He sighed. "After we located the *Puthaid*."

"Och, making it clear the ship comes first?"

Pedr frowned. "She's already mentioned that, Uncle. Shall we find something else to discuss? I'll likely need the rest of the day to correct my mistake."

Laird MacNeill cleared his throat. "Are we in accord?"

Pedr raised a brow, the man's desire to be shed of his daughter irritating him mightily. "Ye heard yer daughter. She has agreed to be my wife. Do ye make it a habit to seek confirmation of yer daughter's opinion from others? I assure ye, 'tis nae how to deal with her."

The laird waved a hand. "Bah. She'll do as she's told. I ask if ye're still of a mind to marry her or if ye've decided to cry off now that ye've spent a gey wheen of time alone with her."

Pedr slapped his palms to the worn surface of the laird's desk. "Let it be known, auld man, that this is the last time ye will have a say in yer daughter's life. We shall wed on the morrow, and, as my wife, will then be under *my* protection. Are we clear?"

"Och, dinnae fash. 'Tis time she was wed and nae longer my concern." He leveled a finger at Pedr. "But dinnae cry foul when she balks at doing her duty like a proper lass. I've done my best to raise her and never seen the likes of a woman carryin' on like she does. *Cannae bear to be ashore*, she says. *Wants to be aboard a ship*."

He grabbed a thin piece of parchment, often scraped for re-use, though ink stains remained. With a shaking hand, he dipped a goose quill in a small tub of ink.

Pedr placed a finger atop the parchment. "I'll pen the contract if ye dinnae mind."

Laird MacNeill handed over the quill and parchment, and with a careful hand, Pedr wrote:

Pedr MacLean and Rona MacNeill

by which Pedr MacLean, second son of Baron Birk MacLean of Morvern, undertakes to marry Rona MacNeill, only child of Laird Galen MacNeill of the Isle of Gigha, on December 21, the year of our Lord, 1300.

Laird Galen MacNeill will provide, in lieu of dowry, information leading to the recovery of the ship, Puthaid, that it may be returned to Pedr MacLean and MacLean Shipping , before the beginning of Yule, this same year.

For Rona's sake—and to hopefully win a few points in his favor—Pedr added a creative bit about the bride price, payable only to her in the event of any dissolvement of their marriage, and promising to honor, provide for, and support her. He did not add any part that would implicate the MacLean clan as more than allies with the MacNeills, not wishing for such to be discovered in print and boasting his signature. He would not go so far without his da's consent.

With such embellishments as he could manage with the ancient quill and well-used parchment, he then sanded the document before passing it to his uncle for approval.

Sten adjusted the length of his arm, then scanned the hastily penned notice. After a second glance, he passed it to Laird MacNeill.

Pedr met MacNeill's glower with a shrug. "Ye're getting what ye wanted. Yer daughter off yer hands in exchange for my ship. 'Tis clear the *Puthaid* came through Ardminish Harbor. Be happy I dinnae demand the return of the stores and livestock aboard the ship as well." He pinned the man with a pointed stare. "Or, have ye arrested for knowingly allowing my ship to pass through yer hands."

He scooped up the parchment and handed it back to Sten. "Ye'll stand witness, aye?"

Sten nodded. "If 'tis what ye wish."

"Aye. Keep a close watch on the contract, uncle. I'm off to make amends with my bride."

Chapter Eight

Rona took the steps two at a time but could not outdistance the fact Pedr agreed to marry her only to get his ship back. Murdo's nails clicked on the stone as he trotted at her heels.

I dinnae wish my marriage to be one of convenience—for him!

She opened the door to her room, putting her strength behind its grinding protest, silently cursing all things—human, wooden, and otherwise—standing in her way. She stomped inside the chamber then dragged her surcoat over her head and unlaced her kirtle, too upset to heed the hen flesh rising on her arms in the cold room. The wind flung sleet against the keep with an icy hiss, rattling the slender wooden shutter in the single window.

Murdo leapt to the bed and turned twice before burrowing into the blanket, then peered at her through a white fringe of hair, his dark, round eyes following her every move.

Rona quickly slipped into leggings and a worn woolen tunic, exchanging her half-boots for heavier footwear, then slouched onto the mattress next to the little terrier.

"What do ye think, *cù beag?* I've had two days to consider marriage, and scarcely an hour to consider Pedr MacLean as my husband."

She scratched Murdo's chin. He whined. Rona sighed and leaned against a bedpost. "Aye, he's easy on the eyes, though I wouldnae have noticed if Da hadnae insisted I wed him."

Murdo yipped. Rona chuckled. "Och, mayhap I would

have noticed. Arms and shoulders strong enough to keep a ship steady on course in the roughest seas . . ..”

“Rugged good looks—which I got from my ma, ye may be interested to know. She's Welsh.”

Rona whirled, her heart racing. Pedr leaned against the doorframe—which she'd neglected to shut, or at least, hadn't shoved closed. Murdo growled then leapt from the bed with a bark. He raced across the floor and skidded to a halt at Pedr's feet. Sniffing his boots, he circled the intruder. Pedr eyed him benevolently. Even clucked invitingly—and the wee skunner wagged his stumpy tail.

Rona scowled. “And enough audacity to think he can get his way without challenge.”

Pedr tilted his head. “Do ye plan to challenge me?”

“Is yer ma truly Welsh?”

He chuckled. “Aye. And a lot like ye.”

“Oh?”

“She'd sooner skewer my da as argue with him—and he knows he'd come out on the losing end of that engagement. But she's fair and caring and would give ye the last bit of silver in her pocket if ye needed it.” Pedr shifted his weight to his other shoulder. “She and her first husband fought in the Welsh Wars of Independence. He died around a year before Longshanks's army beat the Welsh at the Battle of Orewin Bridge. She and her brother fled north, and she lost him in a storm which cast her ashore along the Ardnamurchan Peninsula, on MacLean land.”

“I like that she opposes Longshanks.” Rona shook her head. “Such loss could have embittered her. She must be a strong woman.”

“Aye, she is. She even managed to pull my ama to her side when they were introduced.”

“To her side? What do ye mean?”

Pedr's grin slipped. “She . . . er . . . wed my da under unusual circumstances, and he'd not sent word to Morvern—

and his ma—of their marriage. Ama thought she was my elder sisters'—who were verra young at the time—new nurse."

"An inauspicious introduction." Rona shifted her balance on the mattress, drawing one leg up to counter the weight on her other leg. "What will yer ma say when ye bring a bride home . . . unannounced?"

A grin split Pedr's face. "She'll say I'm just like my da. Then probably box my ears."

Pedr couldn't help staring at his soon-to-be bride. No delicate lass, his Rona, she embodied the fire and tenacity and courage he'd told Alex and Brant he looked for in a wife. He could be gone long months at sea and not worry how she or his home and family fared.

Then, why did he suddenly feel as if he'd bitten into a sour plum?

He eyed her leggings and tunic. "I like the change. Are ye nae comfortable in a gown?"

"I have much to do and 'tis is easier to accomplish them dressed like this." She glanced at her clothing then back at him. "I dinnae like wedding ye to get yer ship back. I'll tell ye where to look for her. Ye dinnae have to go through with the marriage."

Pedr worked his lips to a pained, regretful grimace. "I dinnae mean it the way it sounded earlier. I must bring the ship back, and I will be pleased to present ye to my family as soon as we return to Morvern—and they *will* give ye a grand feast. But getting the ship isnae why I'll marry ye tomorrow."

She arched a brow, pale against the rich hue of her wind-kissed skin. "Why? We've only just met. Ye could have any lass boasting enough years to bear ye a son. If ye're looking for a wife to sit at home and embroider, and happy to see ye come through the door after a month or more at sea, ye'll be sorely disappointed in me."

That was the problem—and slap him with a salmon for not realizing it earlier! He did not want a wife who sat at home whilst he traveled. Alex might be content to have his wife fulfill the role of lady of the castle. Pedr wanted a different life.

"Why settle on *me*? *Now*?" Her frown deepened.

"I may marry whom I wish. Why *not* ye?" he countered.

"Ye are young. Why wed now?"

It was Pedr's turn to scowl. "I am of age . . .."

"Da mentioned yer brother has taken a bride. Do ye wish merely to parade me as proof ye can take a wife as well?"

Pedr didn't like her accusation, or her tone. "He and I oft have the same thoughts, desires." He lifted one shoulder. "Da has tasked us with finding brides before Yule. He believes Alex and I are of an age and accomplishments whereby marriage is the next logical step."

"Ye would marry me to fulfill yer da's command?"

"Ye have a choice, may I remind ye. A pirate may be punished by hanging. As my wife, ye'd be above suspicion."

Rona tapped her toe against the bare wood floor. "Yer noose or the bailiff's?

Pedr tilted his head, ire fading to admiration. "Is there naught ye fear?"

"Truth? The only thing I fear is fading into a life of non-existence. I havenae the heart for a life ashore, waiting for my husband to return from the sea."

"Would ye prefer to travel with me? Learn to barter and trade with people who dinnae speak yer language? To see places ye've nae heard of before? Bear our children in far-off lands with the rise and fall of the waves beneath yer bed?"

Her eyes gleamed. Avarice? Lust? He clearly had exceeded her expectations. It was a heady mixture which sent his blood singing hot through his veins as if he'd quaffed the finest whisky.

She tossed him a half-smile. "I believe I'd even give up pirating for life aboard ship."

He roared with laughter. "I'll nae bail ye from the bailiff's court should ye be caught pirating. I drive a hard bargain, but I'm an honest merchant."

She grinned. "Then I shall be above reproach, and nae besmirch yer name."

His mood soared. "Come. We've a contract to sign and a wedding to prepare for."

Next day

Pedr ordered the *Banríon Laoch* stripped of her stores for the wedding supper, leaving only enough for three days' rations on board, and invited Brant, Haldor and the crew to the keep to join the festivities.

A woman introduced as Rona's aunt had whisked her away the night before, chattering about gowns and the lack of flowers for her hair, and other such female concerns. Pedr glanced at the stairwell for at least the tenth time in as many minutes and was rewarded with the same sight as before. Naught but MacNeill clans people and MacLean sailors milling about, happily swilling ale and anticipating the nuptials.

"She'll nae come down faster for yer willing it, lad," Sten said.

Haldor, ashore for the ceremony—leaving hand-picked warriors aboard the *Banríon Laoch* to protect the ship—laughed. "He's realizing he's about to become shackled to the lass, and isnae certain if he wishes to flee or brazen it out."

"I'm nae two-minded," Pedr replied, his voice more of a growl than he'd intended.

Brant elbowed the captain. "Then he's worried what his ma'll say. Formidable woman, my aunt."

Sten nodded sagely. "I wouldnae wish to fall afoul of her—nor *my* ma." He lifted one shoulder. "They'll be pleased to welcome Lady Rona to the family—and skelp him for following in his da's footsteps."

"Plucking a bride from the gallows. 'Tis a MacLean tradition." Brant's leer nearly earned him a hearty punch, though Pedr was mildly disinclined to start a brawl on his wedding day.

A young man in a friar's robes joined the MacLeans. His face tended toward freckles, and his tonsure was a brilliant red as yet undimmed by age. His smile was as engaging as his appearance.

"I am Henry, Laird MacNeill's nephew." He inclined his head.

"Aren't ye a bit young to have taken vows?" Sten asked, peering at the youngster.

"Och, I've always been destined for the church," he replied, his good humor undaunted by the question. "I've six brothers older than me, and ye may have noted a dearth of land on this isle. I've schooled at Saddell Abbey these past few years and will formally take vows in the spring. I'm home for the Holy Days to visit family. Uncle Galen asked me to look over the bridal contract."

It struck Pedr anew how poor the clan truly was. Time was likely spent harvesting the seas and farming what fertile land they had. The ability to read and write appeared to be of little value to this island clan. He would see that Rona would have access to any tutoring she desired—and offer tutoring for the children of the isle at least during the winter months.

He indicated the worn parchment on the table with a tilt of his head. "I penned it yestereve. It awaits yer approval."

Young Henry retrieved the contract and carefully read the contents, his lips pursed in concentration. "Ye've nae been wed before? 'Tis a nice bit of wording. Rona will like that ye've offered her a means to support herself should ye predecease her."

"Should our marriage end for any reason, the bride price is hers."

The soon-to-be friar nodded. "Ye're a fair man, Pedr MacLean. Ye honor yer sire."

Pedr's brows lifted. "Ye know him?"

"I know of him—enough to tell me he's a bear of a man, yet none have ill words for him. Rona is a lucky woman."

"'Tis my hope ye willnae have to tell her that."

The level of noise in the room shifted. Brant nudged him. Pedr's gaze fell upon the stairs once more. A young woman—recognizable by her high cheek bones, gray eyes, blonde hair, and steady gaze—approached slowly on Laird MacNeill's arm, supporting him as he hobbled painfully across the floor. A gaggle of women clustered around.

She was beautiful. Her aunt—for they were much of a size—must have loaned her a gown and trimmed it in bridal blue, for it did not stretch too tight across her shoulders, nor did it clear the ground well above her ankles. The modestly-cut neckline of her kirtle was also edged in blue, and a necklace with an amethyst the size of his thumbnail—he decided asking its origins would not be prudent—hung from a slender silver chain.

Rona halted before him and he took her hands in his. He leaned close.

"The amethyst symbolizes piety and martyrdom. A subtle protest?"

She quirked a brow. "Nae. I've been told 'tis a stone of peace and a promise of fidelity."

He winged his arm and she placed her palm upon his sleeve. "Then I shall shower ye with amethysts and anything else yer heart desires."

"I require little," she replied as he turned her to the table where the contract awaited.

"I live to bring a smile to yer lips." He shifted his

attention to young Henry. "If ye would be so kind as to read aloud the terms so all gathered might hear them?"

Henry's slight nod told him he'd chosen right to not assume his bride could read. Rona's chin lifted as Henry read the contract, and Pedr was also satisfied to perceive when her startled gaze flicked to his that his generous offer of the bride price had been noted.

Laird MacNeill nodded, fierce concentration on his face. "Good to see ye're learning at the monastery and nae wasting our coin, lad."

Henry raised a brow but didn't miss a beat as he read the final words.

Pedr picked up the quill when Henry set the parchment back to the table and signed his name with only a small flourish.

Rona accepted the quill and penned her name in a steady, though barely legible hand.

"I accept ye as my wife. Will ye accept me as yer husband?"

A hush fell and Pedr glanced over his shoulder as Sten cleared his throat. A sturdy man he did not recognize stood a few feet away, beefy arms crossed over his chest, the area around him cleared of people.

"I object."

Chapter Nine

"Uncle Oran!" Rona took a single step took her in her uncle's direction, but Pedr tightened his arm, trapping her hand against his side.

"Dinnae interfere," Laird MacNeill barked, his sharp gaze leveled at his brother.

"She has a right to be heard, and the last *I* heard, she dinnae wish to wed." Oran's stubbornness matched her da's.

She cast a quick look to Pedr who stood stony-faced at her side, his fingers twitching as though itching to join a fight. His uncle and two other men formed up next to Pedr, shoulders nearly touching.

Please dinnae draw yer sword. She lightly squeezed his forearm, hoping to reassure him, then returned her gaze to Uncle Oran, a pleading tilt to her head. "There's nae need to object, uncle. I dinnae oppose the marriage."

He scowled. "I willnae let Galen send ye away with a man nae of yer choosing. Ye belong with us, Rona. On the sea. Nae stuck away in a croft as some Highlander's brood mare."

"Uncle Oran!" she hissed. Her cheeks heated and her temper flared. "I'll thank ye to nae speak out of turn. Stand down and I'll speak tae ye in a bit."

Oran's wife hurried to his side and clutched his arm as if begging him to silence. Though his flashing eyes told Rona he did not agree, he clamped his mouth shut and offered no further argument.

Rona faced Pedr, feeling the brunt of her uncle's glare as a sharp point between her shoulder blades.

"I accept ye as my husband, from this day forth."

His gaze slid from Oran to her and his face softened. "So be it."

A slow smile spread across his face, crinkling the corners of his eyes, and he lowered his lips to hers. Cheers filled the room. Her breath fled. Her wits scattered on the winds. His fingers tightened about hers. She leaned forward, her breasts lightly touching his chest, sparking a wave of desire that took her completely by surprise.

Pedr drew back. "We . . . we're required at the table." His voice rasped, sending a delightful shiver through her.

So, he'd been affected as well? Satisfaction twisted a corner of her lips. Giving his hands a quick squeeze, she faced the three MacLean men at his side.

They bowed their heads.

"Welcome to the family, Lady Rona," the elder intoned. "I am Sten of Hallstein, young Pedr's uncle." He motioned to the man next to him. "My son, Haldor."

"Uncle Sten's mother is my grandma." Pedr motioned to the third man whose dark eyes danced merrily, the skin crinkled at their corners.

"I am Brant MacCain," the young man said. His red-gold hair glistened in the light of the candles. "Yer husband's da is my uncle. I've fostered with his family these past few years learning the shipping business. If ye have questions about him, ye have but to ask."

Rona hid a grin. "I shall remember that."

Pedr sent Brant a quelling look. Haldor gave Brant's ear a good-natured cuff.

"Ouch! I'm only trying to help." Brant's disgruntled voice drifted to Rona's ears and she swallowed laughter as Pedr led her to the head table.

Murdo trotted at her side as cocky as if he was in charge of the entire feast. A lazy hound drew near, ears nearly dragging the ground as he lowered his head to sniff the little terrier. Certain he was every bit as large as the leggy hound,

Murdo yelped imperiously and made two hops toward the dog on stiffened legs. With a surprised yip, the hound loped from the room, tail between his legs.

With a shake of her head, Rona dismissed the terrier's antics and took her seat. Her heart swelled as she realized Pedr had created an impromptu feast for the MacNeills, the like of which they'd not seen in her lifetime. Plain and simple fare, yet plenty for all—including more of the marmalade like they'd plundered from the *Puthaid*. Bits of greenery, red berries, and white shells graced the head table, reminding Rona Yule was but a few days away.

People laughed and chatted as they ate their fill. Even Oran, his misgivings softened by a bit of ale and clamors for tales of the Black MacNeill, appeared to enjoy the feast. Rona's ears burned as he related their theft of the *Puthaid*, but Pedr seemed bemused by the tale. He shook his head more than once during the telling.

Both Brant and Haldor nudged Sten, demanding explanation, but he merely grinned and shook his head.

Two musicians with pipes and another claiming a passing knowledge with his fiddle warmed up in one corner of the room. The pipes evoked the breathy sound of wind over the stones—rather apt for the clan which lived atop a nearly barren rock. The fiddle, however, made up for his lack of tuning with fervor and volume—and, unfortunately, a large number of songs committed to memory.

The fiddle squawked enthusiastically as the pipes strove for mastery of the tune. Rona bit her lip against a smile as Pedr squinted in what could only have been pain. The MacNeills bellowed the words to the lusty seafaring songs, completely unaware of how far they drifted out of tune.

At last, the fiddler called a break, and a lad with a voice still on the sweet side of puberty stopped before Rona's and Pedr's table and sang.

Of every kinne tre,

Of every kinne tre,
The hawthorn bloweth sweetest,
Of every kinne tre.
My lemman she shal be,
My lemman she shal be,
The fairest of every kinne,
My lemman she shal be.

(*Of every kind of tree, The hawthorn blossoms sweetest. Of every kind of tree, my lover she shall be.*)

Memory of their earlier kisses spread warmth through Rona, reminding her she would be his lover very soon. She sent Pedr a glance, wondering if he entertained the same thoughts. He grinned then pushed his chair back and lifted a much-tarnished quaich which held a clear, un-aged whisky.

Gripping a handle in each hand—offering trust amid a clan he was not bound to except through this marriage, and showing he held no weapons in his hands—he held the silver bowl aloft. "To my bonnie bride. Drink with me and seal the pact of our marriage."

Rona stood and accepted the quaich, both her hands on the handles in her own show of faith. "To my husband." Without hesitation, she tossed back a decent swallow of the raw whisky. Her eyes watered, but she didn't falter, even as the fumes filled her nose and throat and the whisky burned its way down to her stomach.

He accepted the quaich back, draining the dish of all she'd left. His eyes watered, too, but his uncle and cousins pounded his back in manly sympathy. Her Aunt Revna—Uncle Oran's wife—rolled her eyes, a tolerant smile on her lips.

"May there be peace between yer bonds, and love which will take root and grow throughout the long years." She patted Rona's hand. "Yer ma would wish it so."

Words failed Rona. She swallowed hard and blinked

back tears. Ma would not have wished her to become a pirate, nor for her da to hand her over to be wed to a man she scarcely knew. But, she believed her ma would have ultimately approved the match. Peace between herself and Pedr would suffice where she had no expectation of love.

"Thank ye, Aunt Revna," she replied.

Music erupted from the fiddles and pipes, and tables were hastily pushed back to clear the room for dancing. Pedr joined in, laughing as his feet sought the right steps. Brant and Haldor also joined the merriment while Sten watched from the far side of a mug of whisky.

At last, breathing hard but laughing as he caught his breath, Pedr grabbed her hand and dragged her from the merry-making.

"Come with me," he said, pulling her close for a quick kiss. He then edged the room and led her out the door. Taking her cue from her husband, Rona ignored the calls of farewell—and improbable suggestions, weren't they?—from others in the room.

The brisk air took her breath away, but she was still over-warm from her exertions, and followed him as he hurried away from the keep.

"Where are we going?" she asked, lengthening her stride to keep up.

A few minutes later, they stood at the harbor where the *Banríon Laoch* wallowed in the gentle lap of the surf. The sleet from the earlier storm had been cleared away, but the rime-coated bits of metal rigging glistened in the moonlight, and the wood shone with a silver gleam.

"I promised ye the rise and fall of the waves beneath yer bed. Now, and always."

Rona stared at the ship, its tall mast a stain against the night sky. A sudden breeze made her shiver, and she clenched her teeth against their clatter.

"Come. I'll see ye warm in a thrice."

She caught his winsome smile even in the moonlight, and something inexplicable caused her legs to tremble as a new warmth bloomed deep inside. Being cold around her new husband was *not* likely to be a problem.

Guards sent respectful nods as they passed, and cheeky grins when they thought Rona wasn't looking. A pang of embarrassment quickly passed, replaced by a flurry of anticipation.

Their feet thudded softly on the boards. She craned her neck, inspecting the ship, gaze caught by what appeared to be a giant crossbow mounted on the aftcastle.

"What is that?"

Pedr caught her glance and laughed. "I dinnae know wooing my wife would involve explaining a ballista. Though I cannae truly say I'm disappointed." He sent her an admonishing glance tempered with a smile but changed his step and brought them to the weapon.

"Do ye wish for the history, or a brief explanation—or mayhap an exhibition of its power?"

Rona blinked. As fascinating as she found the enormous weapon, Pedr's voice nudged aside her curiosity, reminding her of the reason they'd boarded the ship so late in the evening. In answer, she closed the small distance between them and raised up on her toes. Her kiss fell short of his lips, not from lack of trying, but from lack of height. Pedr quickly made up the difference.

His arms wrapped about her waist, pulling her hard against him. She ran her fingers through his hair, tugging his head closer, his lips more firmly to hers. The kiss deepened, his tongue seeking hers as it plundered her mouth. Her breath shortened even as her heart raced.

Pedr slowly pulled away, resting his cheek against the top of her head.

"I'd make love to ye here beneath the stars and the sea air around us, were it not so blessed cold," he chuckled.

"Mayhap another time."

"Mayhap this ship has a captain's cabin where we could find a spot out of the wind *and* a bit of privacy?"

"Assuredly it does. Though we willnae put Haldor from his chamber. The *Banríon Laoch* boasts two such cabins, and I made certain Brant cleared his belongings out before he came ashore." He led her to the main deck where thin lines of light framed a sturdy wooden door. He opened the portal, and a wash of lamplight spilled across the boards.

Warmth engulfed her as she entered the small but well-appointed chamber. Pedr quickly closed the door, banishing the wintry air. He settled the wooden latch to assure no interruptions. A surge of panic welled up, but Rona quelled it.

"Having second thoughts?"

His question startled her. She hadn't thought she was that transparent. "Nae. I've seen naught from ye that makes me think ye're anything but honorable." She arched a brow. "Devious, mayhap, but I have nae reason to fear ye or our marriage bed."

The creases on his brow smoothed and he took her in his arms once again. His hands rubbed lightly up and down her arms, raising hen flesh on her skin. Her breasts swelled beneath her gown as his thumbs swept across her nipples and she arched against him with a moan. His mouth covered hers hungrily while his fingers deftly loosened her laces so her gown lifted easily over her head. Her thin under gown quickly followed, and she sat on the edge of the wide berth to remove her stockings and shoes.

Her attention quickly diverted as Pedr untied his belt and allowed his trews to fall in a puddle to the floor. His boots joined their growing pile of clothes, and Rona tossed her stockings atop the tangle of wool and linen.

Pedr raised his tunic over his head and sent the dark blue cloth sailing into the shadows. Rona's eyes widened, her own nakedness forgotten as she perused the man before her. His height and the corded power of his arms and legs could have given her pause, but the hard lines of his body, gilded by lamp light, begged her touch. It was more than she imagined. Her gaze slipped.

"I've nae truly looked . . .." She bit her lip before she said something foolish. Like, how much the sight of his strong body turned her own to a quiver of anticipation. Or how much she wanted to touch him, run her hands over the rugged perfection he presented. Or, mayhap, taste him. So many choices, yet she did little more than draw the corner of her lip between her teeth in indecision.

Nae, much better to stare than give voice to inanities such as those flitting through her head. What would he think of her if he knew what she wanted?

"I dinnae mind if ye look, lass," he rumbled, the low timbre of his voice catching her breath. "but I'd prefer ye come touch me."

All of her good intentions vanished, and Rona stepped into his arms.

Chapter Ten

Clouds hung low in the winter sky. Sails snapped briskly in the wind as they awaited Pedr's command to depart. Rona stood on the dock, listening intently to Oran's hurried words. Two of her cousins carried a chest with her clothes and personal effects aboard, and Murdo—after dancing about happily for a few moments upon seeing her—scampered after them.

"I dinnae expect to come home and find ye wed, lass." He shook his head. "Nor leaving us before Yule." He cast a glance at Pedr who waited with his men a few steps away. "He appears a fine lad—mayhap a bit young, but sure of himself and of a good temperament. All know the MacLeans are a powerful clan. Howbeit, ye will send word if ye need me for anything."

"I'm nae worried about Pedr. He is proving to be a good man. His family may be a different matter," she confessed.

"Not certain if they'll approve of a pirate in the family?"

"Och, they've pirates aplenty," she replied with a toss of her head. "They're nae like us, Uncle. 'Twill take some getting used to."

"Ye will do well. I have nae doubt ye will easily win their hearts."

He glanced at Pedr who appeared to have taken an interest in the lads as they set Rona's chest inside the cabin. Lowering his voice, he turned back to Rona.

"I wanted to tell ye of my conversation with the MacDonnell. He bought the ship readily enough, and he was pleased to have it. Paid more than I expected." He hefted a small leather bag then slipped it into Rona's outstretched hand.

She blinked in surprise at the weight. She tugged the drawstring open and peered inside, then handed it back. "Silver? Uncle, 'tis more than I expected. Ye can keep the clan fed this winter and the next with enough to help get crops in the fields come spring. Mayhap more sheep."

Oran tucked the bag out of sight beneath his cloak. "Aye. The MacDonnell's eyes gleamed pure avarice when he saw the ship."

"Do ye believe he knows 'tis a MacLean ship?"

"Och, aye, he does, lassie. And I believe he's counting on MacLean coming for it."

Pedr gave the command to set sail after Oran and his sons took their leave, leaving Brant and Haldor to pester Sten over the truth of his wife's former identity as the Black MacNeill while he joined his wife at the rail. He shook his head, still a bit surprised at the thought he was a married man. And more than a bit bemused his wife had recently been known as the Black MacNeill.

And had stolen his ship.

"We'll reach Islay in a few hours. Will Aonghus Og be expecting us, do ye think?"

The winter wind teased a strand of golden hair loose from Rona's braid, and brought color to her cheeks.

"Aye. At least, he likely hopes ye'll come seeking the *Puthaid*. 'Twill save him the journey."

"Och, if he knows the *Puthaid* is a MacLean ship, he'll nae wait to rub it in our noses that 'tis now his. He wouldnae consider being noble and returning it."

A small snort escaped Rona. "The MacNeills are a bit isolated, but even I know the MacLeans and the MacDonnells arenae allies."

"'Tis a wonder ye sell ships to Aonghus. He's a known supporter of King Edward."

Rona gave a slow nod. "There is rumor he is sympathetic with a man called Robert de Brus who was a guardian of Scotland until his quarrels with Comyn got the better of him. 'Tis a slippery slope Aonghus Og strides. The truth of the matter is, he can afford to pay for the ships, while many others cannae. When ye are poor, ye may find mutual greed suits ye better than political morality."

"Once the MacDonnell knows ye've married a MacLean, the MacNeills will nae longer be able to claim support from him."

"I believe I've chosen the better path." She nudged his arm. "My days of stealing ships are past."

Pedr grinned. "Ye're a reformed woman? I like the woman ye were last night. In my arms. Dinnae reform too much."

A deep blush spread over Rona's cheeks, overtaking the wind's caress. "I rather enjoyed discovering a bit about ye, as well. Shall we continue our studies this eve?"

He nodded. "Aye. That sounds like the best offer I've had in many a day."

"I've only known ye a pair of days," she laughed.

He hugged her close to his side, enjoying the feel of her body against his, distracted by wondering if they could slip away for an hour or two before they reached Islay and Aonghus Og MacDonnell's seat of power.

As tempting as the idea was, he reluctantly discarded it. "We'll arrive on Islay at Port Askaig, put in ashore, and make the overland trip to Loch Finlaggan. Doubtless, we'll be intercepted at the harbor and escorted to Eilean Mor."

"The MacDonnells have quite a settlement on the loch. I've nae been there, but Uncle Oran has—to sell the ships."

"'Tis well-known they've a gey wheen of influence and wealth in the isles. We will be firmly within MacDonnell fortifications and might."

"Does that bother ye?"

Pedr tilted his head, then lifted a shoulder. "I'm more worried about having the funds to buy my ship back. Aonghus Og willnae let her go for a mere pittance."

"Nae. He willnae."

They remained at the rail a few moments. Pedr relished the salt air—and the coming reckoning. "How much did the MacDonnell pay for the ship?"

"I dinnae count the silver, but 'twas a hefty amount."

"Hmm. He must anticipate making up for it by ransoming it back to us for an outrageous sum."

"'Twould be my guess."

Pedr liked that her voice held no trace of apology.

Rona leaned closer. "The cost of a ship is steep. Have ye such a sum with ye to barter with?"

"Och, dinnae fash. Let's hear what he has to say first."

The *Banríon Laoch* drew to harbor at Port Askaig amid birlinns and sturdy fishing boats. The *Puthaid* was not among them. As Pedr expected, he was allowed to disembark with three soldiers. Rona and Sten joined him after some discussion. He was not happy to bring Rona into the maw of the MacDonnell stronghold, but there was no holding her back.

Brant viewed the procedings with a disgruntled air. "I can help ye, Pedr. Ye know 'tis true."

"I need ye aboard the ship," Pedr said firmly. "'Tis of greater import to have ye and Haldor here, protecting the ship, than add another sword where it willnae be allowed." He offered Brant a sympathetic smile. "We're likely to need yer talents here."

Conceding the argument, Brant remained aboard the *Banríon Laoch,* with a watchful eye on those sharing the harbor.

Pedr and Rona and the other MacLeans seated themselves warily in a wagon drawn by shaggy-coated ponies, and were escorted over the well-worn road inland. Less than an hour's ride brought them to Loch Finlaggan, sheltered at the base of hillocks, with two crannogs—islands made by men—sitting in the placid gray-blue waters.

Pedr hopped from the wagon as it halted near the edge of the loch and helped Rona down to continue their journey on foot. He passed a large standing stone and stared down the valley at the very heart of the MacDonnell rule.

Prickly furze lined the loch, its evergreen leaves frosted with a light dusting of snow. Pedr's breath hung white in the air a moment before disappearing. Stepping carefully around the spiny shrubs, he and Rona crossed a stone bridge stretching from the shore to the larger of the two islands, known as Eilean Mor.

They then passed through the wooden fortifications on the north end of the crannog which encircled what appeared to be planting areas lying fallow for the season. Few people were out in the cold, only two days before Yule, and they eyed Pedr and his men with only mild distrust before returning to their chores.

Sten stepped close to Pedr and Rona. "'Tis fortunate MacLean shipping doesnae need to travel south of Islay. There is a long history of Norse and Gael warriors prowling these waters. Loch Indaal, on the southern shore, is the perfect harbor, but of little use to any who dinnae align with the MacDonnell and his ilk."

"'Tis likely where the *Puthaid* is harbored," Rona said. "'Tis well-protected once ye round Laggan point. I saw it once not too many months ago."

Pedr shot her a grin of delight, knowing she'd been here to sell a stolen English ship. She shrugged, a twinkle lighting her eyes.

"I believe ye are right," Sten replied. "He wouldnae have had a chance to take the ship elsewhere—especially since I daresay he wasnae expecting us so soon."

They paused as the MacDonnells halted the procession at the final gate before continuing to a large stone keep that guarded the landscape.

Pedr eyed his uncle. "Before ye joined Da—when ye were a pirate—yer ships sailed from Kiloran Bay on Colonsay, aye?"

Sten rubbed his chin. "Aye. One of the isles claimed by Aonghus Og. For a time, King Alexander could do naught with the Norse, and left us alone." His eyes glittered beneath beetled brows. "I sought revenge on those who had destroyed my village and killed my family—which seemed to suit the MacDonnell, for he did naught about our piracy except occasionally remember to demand a tithe. When Ma found me on Colonsay, I was eventually convinced to change my ways."

Rona raised her brows but said naught.

"Aonghus Og has a long arm," Pedr said. "Da occasionally disputes the ownership of the Ardnamurchan Peninsula with him."

"Somerled's sons claim much of the Isles and western shores."

Pedr gave a jerk of his chin to the stone and wood buildings on the crannog. "They've quite a settlement here. 'Twould take an immense force to oust them. Simple to hold or destroy the bridge, and, without a host of birlinns to ply the loch, their enemy could do little more than stand on the shore and shake their fists."

Sten nodded agreement. "Whilst their ships sit in harbors too far away to be of help."

They were granted entrance to the great hall where a fire blazed in the hearth and people bustled about. A few relaxed in chairs near the fire. A large man, eyes glittering beneath heavy auburn brows, beckoned Pedr, Rona, and Sten closer.

He stood and inclined his head to Rona. "Welcome to Finlaggan. My messenger is to be commended, it seems. I sent him out just yester eve and already MacLean has sent people for his ship—though I dinnae expect a woman."

Pedr ground his teeth yet managed a half-smile. "Lady Rona is my wife." He took a firmer grip on his temper. "'Twould seem yer reputation precedes ye, m'lord, for I left Morvern well ahead of the arrival of yer messenger. I'd hoped not to find a MacLean ship in the hands of the MacDonnell, but . . .." His grin hardened.

Aonghus Og glanced up and down Pedr, dismissing Sten with only a cursory look. "I hope ye've the authority to make an offer for the ship."

"I am, alas, only his younger son," Pedr replied, knowing full well the man knew who he was. "But I have enough authority to offer ye what ye paid the Black MacNeill for the ship. Piracy is frowned upon in some quarters."

The MacDonnell shrugged expansively, his face a study in innocence. "I've nae hand in piracy. We are a peaceful clan."

And rule these waters with an iron fist. Pedr had no delusions about the power and might of the MacDonnell chief.

Neither spoke for a long moment, then the MacDonnell waved to the nearby tables. "We are about to partake of our noon meal. Please, sit with us."

Pedr hesitated, eager to retrieve the ship and be home. Bypassing the offer, however, was not possible without causing offense. If they sat at the MacDonnell board, wouldn't they be safe enough?

Chapter Eleven

The whisky was excellent, with the hint of salty sea air Pedr expected from spirits distilled near the sea. The fare had been abundant and well-presented, with no cost spared. Pedr leaned back in his chair as the room cleared and gave his host a polite smile.

"I thank ye for yer hospitality. The cold makes my belly rumble."

Aonghus Og waved a hand. "'Twas naught. The Yule celebrations will begin in two days. The feasting and drinking will last long into the night." He chuckled. "Likely several nights. We will have tumblers and music and competitions to entertain us. Already, the nobles and their families and servants, craftsmen, and churchmen have gathered on the shores of Finlaggan." He rose. "Come. We have business to attend."

He led the way across the hall. Pulling his heavy wool cloak close, he awaited them at the door. "We will retire to the Council Island where we should find a bit of privacy."

Pedr, Rona, Sten, and their soldiers, traversed the causeway between the two isles and entered the small stone building where councils were held. A fire had been recently laid, but the room remained cold, and Pedr noticed Rona's shiver. Without a word, he removed his cloak and placed it about her shoulders.

The MacDonnell chief seated himself in an ornate chair at the head of the large table. He did not invite Pedr or his followers to sit. Armed MacDonnell retainers lined the chamber. In this room where weighty matters were decided by a council of powerful chieftains, Pedr felt the walls close in.

He should not have allowed Rona to come.

"I have a sum for ye for the return of yer ship." Aonghus Og named a staggering figure.

Pedr was glad he gripped the back of the chair before him, for his knees trembled. "Would I have such a sum with me, my ship would be sunk beneath the waves with the weight," he replied drily. "I could point out having a new ship built would cost us far less."

"Might I mention I would still possess the *Puthaid*? Och, renaming it the *Pèileag* did not keep me from noting the lines typical of a MacLean ship. I cannae decide if I'd rather keep the new name or flaunt the auld one." He raised his eyebrows. "I'll admit I've wanted a MacLean ship for some time now. Though, I'm willing to sell it back to ye."

"For an outlandish price!" Rona scoffed.

Pedr placed his hand gently atop hers and gave it a light squeeze. He agreed, but it would not benefit them to begin a heated argument in a room filled with armed men.

He did not glance at Rona, but answered the MacDonnell. "A price I dinnae carry in my hold. I am willing to part with the sum ye paid the MacNeill pirate and mayhap a bit more for the inconvenience this has caused ye. The price ye quoted is too high."

"I think yer da will pay it."

Pedr shook his head. "He willnae."

Aonghus Og's eyes narrowed and he leaned forward. "He will pay it to ransom the ship—and his son."

Rona bristled. "Ye . . .." Again Pedr squeezed her hand. She squeezed back, struggling to keep her outrage in check. If he had a plan, she did not wish to bungle it.

"Guards!"

MacDonnell soldiers surrounded them at their chief's command, the slip of swords from scabbards harsh in the air.

Pedr's men glanced to him, hands on sword hilts, clearly outnumbered. A low growl rumbled from Sten's chest.

"Ye would break the rules of hospitality?" Pedr's eyes flashed in warning.

"I merely satisfy a business arrangement. Collateral for a price unpaid."

Pedr's chest rose and fell in deep, even breaths, and Rona knew how brittle his hold was—and that her presence was likely the only thing keeping him from plunging into a fight.

MacDonnell soldiers closed in, motioning for them to move toward a door in the far corner of the room.

She could not move. Would *not* walk toward that door and certain imprisonment.

"Faint," Pedr hissed in her ear.

She sent him a startled look, her question cut short by the fierceness of his command and the savage gleam in his eyes.

Without a word, she crumpled to the floor.

"Rona!"

Pedr caught her an instant before her head hit the wooden boards. Silent, eyes closed, taking as shallow breaths as she could manage, Rona remained limp in his arms.

"Ye must let her go. Yer argument is with me."

No answer came from the MacDonnell chief.

"Grant her safe passage back to our ship," Pedr demanded. "Allow her to carry word to my father."

She stirred with a slight moan, telling Pedr she disagreed with his plan. But she would not argue with him. Not yet.

Pedr patted her cheek. "'Tis well, *mo leannan.* Dinnae fash."

My love? Startled, she almost missed Aonghus Og's next words.

"I will send three of my men with her. They will authenticate what she says—or deny any lies."

Rona forced her shout of rage into a hiccup of revival. With a wiggle of protest, she stirred in Pedr's arms. His dark eyes bored into hers, forcing her to understand her role. She gave a sigh of acceptance.

"Can ye rise?" Pedr asked as solicitously as possible. At her nod, he lifted her gently to her feet. "*Mo chridhe,* Chief MacDonnell has decided to spare ye the indignities of imprisonment and has offered to send ye home with an offer for my and our men's release. Do ye need a rest before ye travel?"

Painting her in a delicate light? Calling her *his heart*? Whatever was he up to? If Aonghus Og thought her capable of stirring up trouble, would he recind his offer and keep her where he knew she would not confound his plans? Her new husband appeared to be as cunning as he was braw.

The MacDonnell chief would learn his mistake the hard way—even if it was the last thing she ever did.

"I . . . I believe I can go now," she replied unsteadily. Pedr led her to a chair then drew another close and sat beside her, her hands in his, cheek near hers. Rona raised her voice enough for the MacDonnell to hear. "Does the chief have an offer drawn up I might carry with me? We must be clear with his intent, and I fear . . . .." She raised a hand to her cheek. "I fear I couldnae remember all of it."

The MacDonnell barked an order at a nearby soldier. He returned several minutes later with parchment and an ink well. Quickly, the only sound in the room was the rasp of the quill.

"Dinnae linger," Pedr commanded, his voice low. "Haldor and Brant will see ye home and give the proper introductions. My da will handle things." He brushed her cheek with his lips. "Dinnae fash, *mo chridhe*. All will be well."

Panic fisted her chest. All might *not* be well. She knew it as well as did he, and quailed to think of their time together ending so abruptly. She swallowed against the possibility, and managed a weak smile, surprised at the enormous tug on her heart.

"I trust ye, *elskan mín.* This will end well for us." She buried her face against his neck. "I swear it."

Rona bided her time until she and MacDonnell's men were aboard ship, warding off Haldor's questions with a shake of her head while Brant scowled from a spot at the helm.

"We must make for Morvern with word from Chief MacDonnell," she said. Placing her back to the MacDonnells, she mouthed at Haldor, "*Guard them.*"

Haldor's face expressed a gamut of words and emotions, but he ordered the sails set and drew away from the dock and north into the Sound of Islay.

Maintaining her fragile guise proved difficult, but, if the ship's captain obeyed her without question, it might prompt the MacDonnell men to lower their guard.

It must have worked, for when they reached the open waters beyond Islay and Jura, Rona dropped her pretense and ordered the men disarmed and clapped into chains—much to their surprise.

"Aonghus Og has betrayed us." Anger trembled in her words as she related the events to Haldor and Brant. "He willnae trade with us and has imprisoned Pedr, Sten, and the others, hoping to gain in ransom from Baron MacLean what Pedr couldnae grant him in fair coin. Turn the ship about."

Haldor swore. Brant sent her a startled look. "Are we nae sailing to Morvern with a message for the Baron?"

"*Ye* will return to Port Askaig but linger just out of sight of MacDonnell's men. 'Tis my thought to join ye there."

"And *ye*?"

"Set me ashore as inland as ye can on Loch Gruinart on the western shore. 'Tis a bit of a trip afoot, but I can be at

Black Rock on Loch Indaal by nightfall."

"What do ye plan to do at Black Rock? They will only allow ye to return to Finlaggan under guard."

"I willnae return to Finlaggan." She grinned, her eyes crinkling with anticipation. "Did we nae agree the *Puthaid* is most likely harbored on Loch Indaal?"

Haldor shook his head. "I dinnae like it. Pedr willnae like it. Nor will Sten. 'Tis dangerous."

"Of course 'tis dangerous. 'Tis why they willnae expect it." She stalked toward the captain's cabin. "I've stolen the *Puthaid* once. It shouldnae be difficult to do so again."

"Absolutely not!" Haldor roared as she slammed the door shut. He was still fuming when she opened the door several minutes later after changing her gown for her black leggings, tunic and cape.

Mouth agape, he stared at her. Brant crossed his arms over his chest, frowing as if he meant to have a say in what she attempted. She tilted her head, eyebrows raised in question. "Have ye turned the ship about?"

Haldor's lips firmed into a scowl. "I willnae allow ye to do this. 'Tis folly to think ye can steal a ship from the MacDonnell's harbor."

"Ye have no say in what I can or cannae do," she pointed out. "Ye answer to me."

"I answer to Pedr MacLean!" Haldor shouted.

"Who isnae here."

She met Haldor's gaze evenly.

"Ye cannae do this by yerself."

"I will take four men. More will only hinder me."

A muscle leapt in Haldor's jaw. "Agreed."

Brant stepped before her. "I will go."

His dark eyes flashed in his youthful face. Rona hesitated, doubting his ability to follow her orders. Finally, she nodded assent.

Haldor gave the order to set a southern course following

the western coastline of Islay. He turned back to Rona, a mixture of disbelief and respect on his face.

"By Saint Andrew, ye *are* the Black MacNeill."

Chapter Twelve

It took Rona longer than she expected to complete the trek from the head of Loch Gruinart to the broad beach at the north end of Loch Indaal. The men accompanying her kept up easily, the cold wind seeming to not bother them in the slightest, though Brant's pale skin pinked darkly under the weather's onslaught. Anonymous forms in their dark cloaks, they strode beside her with a rollicking pace betraying their years at sea.

"Do ye have a plan?" Brant asked.

Rona allowed a short nod, not wasting breath on a response.

"Would ye share it?" the young man persisted.

She tossed him a dark look in reply and received a sulky—though silent—answer. Rona sighed. At least the other three did not see the need to chatter.

She halted a short distance from the loch, ducking behind a large rock to take stock of the activity at the shore. The men hunkered down on either side.

"There's the *Puthaid*," she breathed, pointing to a ship tied to the dock at its farthest reach.

"Aye," Brant agreed. "I know her lines. She's a beauty."

They each studied the shore.

"Nae a lot of activity . . .." one of them noted.

"Though 'tis nae unusual this time of year," another replied.

"Nae much call for the fishing fleet to go out . . .."

"And most are ashore readying for . . .."

"Yule."

Rona shook her head, slightly dizzy from the words

rattling from one man to the other. "I'm counting on many of the guards joining the feasting for the High Days," she said, making note of the hut with smoke rising from the thatched roof, and the five men huddled around a small fire on the beach. Smoke hung low in the sky, heralding a coming storm, but, to Rona's relief, the clouds did not appear ready to drop just yet. Bad weather was a problem to deal with later. After they stole the *Puthaid.*

She turned her back to the rock and sat, catching the four men beside her with a sweep of her gaze. "There's a rowboat dragged ashore just this side of that large birlinn. 'Tis likely a tender for the larger ships. We'll use it to circle behind the ships and approach the *Puthaid*, using the birlinn as cover. I will climb aboard and man the rudder. Brant will come with me."

He sent her a startled look.

"The others will free the ropes at the dock," she continued, "then prepare to tow the *Puthaid* through the loch until we reach open waters. The storm clouds should help cover the moon and hide us—most of the time."

She glanced over her shoulder. Thank Saint Columba, the *Puthaid* was too large to beach like the galleys and *nyvaigs*. Storm clouds or not, they would have garnered too much attention attempting to push the ship into the loch.

After a moment, the men nodded acceptance of her plan.

"What if we encounter someone aboard the ship?" Brant asked.

"We will hope there are none aboard." She dropped her hand to one of the long-handled dirks Haldor had given her. "Howbeit, if necessary, we will deal with them." She drew her black scarf over her head.

The men stared at her.

"What?"

Brant chuckled softly. "Damn, but if'n ye arenae the Black MacNeill!"

Wedged once again in the gap between the stern and rudder, Rona made her way up the stern of the *Puthaid*. The dirks gave good purchase, though her fingers cramped in the bitter cold, and she lost her grip on the leather-wrapped handles twice. Moving with care, she scooted slowly upward until she reached the railing and climbed aboard.

She crouched in the shadow of the rail, listening for the tell-tale tramp of boots, or the low murmur of voices. The *Puthaid* creaked as she rolled atop the languid waves near the shore, but otherwise remained as silent as a ghost ship. Finally satisfied she was the only soul aboard, Rona rose and secured the rope ladder to the rail posts with a round turn and two half hitches. Brant climbed nimbly aboard and immediately set about checking the cabin and below decks.

It seemed hours before she heard the muted slap of oars as the other MacLeans slipped past in the rowboat and the rope at the stern pulled taut. Slowly, the *Puthaid* made progress away from the dock. The flames of the fire on the beach grew smaller with each stroke of the oars, and Laggan Point loomed near in the growing darkness. The waves grew larger, cresting white, and the ship's furled sail slapped against the single mast in answer to the wind's challenge.

The faint splash of oars ceased. The *Puthaid* drifted past the rowboat and the three men climbed the ladder and joined Rona and Brant.

"Are we pirates now?" one asked with a grin.

Rona silenced him with a gesture toward the mast. The wind caught the sail with a snap as he unfurled the woolen cloth, and Rona glanced over her shoulder, knowing they were too far away to be easily heard. Movement on the shore tripled the beat of her heart. A shout stole her breath.

"Hoist the sail, lads, and dinnae mind the noise. We've been spotted."

Pedr minded his tongue and controlled his anger as long as he could, giving Rona time to get away. Aonghus Og left him and his men to the mercies of the MacDonnell soldiers, and they were herded to a stone hut just beyond the council building which boasted a small main room and an even smaller chamber with a large metal lock on the latch.

Fury rose, and Pedr kicked the door once it closed behind them, but it did nothing to relieve his temper.

"Bastard! 'Twill be a bloody battle once Da discovers the MacDonnell's treachery."

"Any chance Brant's da would sway the MacDonnell? The MacCains have a solid Norse alliance."

"I doubt Da would spare the time to send word to Uncle James." Pedr shook his head. "Our best hope is Rona and Brant can keep him from outright war."

"Yer sire would fare better to pay the ransom and take his vengeance elsewhere," Sten said. "This isnae a place he's likely to conquer, and the MacDonnell chief knows it."

"When have ye know my da to back down from a challenge? This is about honor, nae about who will win."

"Mayhap yer ma will be able to persuade him to moderation," Sten replied, though his voice held little hope. Birk MacLean was a man who did nothing by halves.

"There are too many ways off the isle. Loch Indaal isnae so far, nor is Loch Guinart. Both cut deep into Islay. Yer da would have to bring enough ships to block all harbors—and even then there are likely those I dinnae know of."

"Shite." Pedr rubbed his hand through his hair. "I must stop him—and I must give Rona time to escape."

Sten glanced around the chamber, hands on his hips. "I can think of a score of places I'd rather be."

The room grew darker as time passed. Pedr clenched and unclenched his fist.

"It has been long enough, do ye agree, uncle?"

Sten heaved a sigh and rose from the floor with a groan. "My auld bones dinnae appreciate the cold. Tell me, nephew. What is yer plan?"

Pedr eyed his uncle, knowing better than to offer a hand to help him rise, but concerned, nonetheless. "We've played the fainting ploy, and Aonghus Og wouldnae likely care if ye succumbed to a heart ailment. I've a bit more value to him, though who's to say how much. Nae, I think an all-out brawl is what's needed here." He spoke to one of his soldiers. "Alan, call for the guards—and make it sound desperate."

With a hefty dose of drama, Alan sounded the alarm. Shouts came from the other room. Alan pounded the door. A key turned in the lock.

Pedr drew back his fist and connected soundly with his uncle's jaw as the door opened. Sten stumbled back, into the arms of the other two MacLean soldiers. He regained his footing and licked at the blood at the corner of his mouth.

"*Fífl. Megi tröllin taka þig.*" Sten growled and his eyes flashed with the spirit of battle an instant before a grim smile split his beard.

Pedr was hard-pressed to keep his fists up and not succumb to laughter. He deserved to be called a fool for striking his uncle, but Sten's subsequent wish that trolls would take him nearly doubled him in mirth.

Sten's swift jab brought Pedr's humor to an abrupt halt. Pain blossomed across his cheek bone, the force of the blow snapping his head to the side.

Four MacDonnell soldiers rushed inside the room, shouting for the men to cease fighting. Pedr bounced back, light on his feet, knees bent. He gestured with one fist.

"*Tyr*!"

Acting on the Norse war cry, Sten stepped toward Pedr then immediately spun about. Back-to-back, he and Pedr launched at the MacDonnells, the MacLeans making short work of subduing their captors. The MacLeans relieved the unconscious men of their swords and Pedr hastily stuffed a dirk in his belt before joining the others as they swept through the open portal. He dabbed a spot above his right eye and discovered a gash he didn't remember receiving. Ignoring the wound, he paused with his uncle at the cottage door.

"'Twill be difficult to retrace our steps over the causeways," Sten mentioned as he took in the surroundings. He glanced at Pedr. "Took a blow, did ye?"

Pedr lightly fingered the gash. "'Tis naught."

Sten grunted and tore a strip from the bottom of his tunic and wrapped it about Pedr's head. "That should keep it from bleeding into yer eyes."

"Thank ye. Ma'll do it up proper later. Let's search the shore for a boat," Pedr suggested. "I dinnae think we'll get off this island the way we came."

With the festivities drawing all the clans of the Isles to Eilean Mor, Pedr and his men soon found an unguarded coracle, its round frame made of saplings and covered with animal hides and large enough for them all.

They pushed off and made the north-west shore as the sun dropped below the horizon. Shouts could be heard in the distance.

"Do ye think they've spotted us?" Alan asked.

"Nae. They've found the guards we left lying on the floor," Sten replied. "Keep yer head down and stay off the main road. If we can make the northern coast, we mayhap can find another boat to make the crossing to Jura."

"'Tis nae much of a swim, if the tide is slack," Pedr noted.

"Swimming the Sound would be my last choice," Sten said reprovingly.

"Nae my choice in mid-winter," Pedr agreed. "But neither is being returned to the MacDonnell."

Chapter Thirteen

Excitement surged through Rona, riding high over the fear of capture. Her heart sang to be so alive—at sea with a challenge so near.

A sleek galley scraped its shallow belly over the sandy beach, its stern rising and dipping as it reached the water of the loch.

"Full sail!" she shouted. Skimming the rudder through the water, she found the current. Wind filled the sail, sending the *Puthaid* plunging past the quiet waters of Loch Indaal and into the storm-chopped waves of the open sea.

The galley's oars ground against the rowlocks, alerting Rona, the sound all but hidden by the flap of sails and splash of waves against the hull of the *Puthaid.* She cast a glance over her shoulder and saw the galley slip over the surface of the loch, oars slicing the water cleanly, increasing its speed. A large wave pounded the *Puthaid's* starboard hull, forcing the ship westward and dousing the crew with a spray of icy sea water. Rona rode the rolling wave with the ease of long practice, letting the *Puthaid* fight her way clear.

"Will ye sail for Morvern?" Brant asked, raising his voice to be heard over the rising wail of the wind.

"Nae. We are to meet Haldor near Port Askaig. From there we will consider how to rescue the others."

He nodded. "Good. I dinnae care to run from these pirates." He sent her an apologetic look. "Beggin' yer pardon."

Rona laughed. "Ye dinnae wish to return to Morvern without the Baron's son!"

Brant grinned as a surge of sea water doused the deck

then swirled back into the depths. "I wasnae certain I liked ye, Lady Rona, though 'twas merely the fact ye'd stolen a MacLean ship and gained a good deal because of it."

"And now?"

"Ye are exactly the wife Pedr needs."

"Why?"

Brant laughed and Rona recognized the same reckless passion she felt. "Because ye stole a MacLean ship!"

He gave a short bow then stood next to her, ready to take the rudder when she tired. "The galley will catch us afore we round the southwesterly point. Give me the helm so ye can return later whilst we fend off the MacDonnells."

Arms strained from fighting the rough seas, Rona gave him possession of the rudder. A shout from below decks caught her attention and she leapt to her feet. Two men hurried up the ladder and approached.

"We've found quicklime!" Feet braced against the roll of the deck, hair plastered to their heads with sea spray, the men appeared pleased with themselves.

They cut the string tying the oiled skins and pulled them away from four small clay jars, each the size of a loaf of bread. The urns were sealed tight against the weather, but the men were careful, nonetheless.

Rona frowned. They had little beyond a few axes and dirks on board, and the MacDonnell sailors likely had swords, giving them the advantage. Quicklime could be the weapon they needed. 'Twas a cruel tactic and she did not relish its use.

There was time. As long as she did not lead them to Haldor and his ship, mayhap they could use the storm to their advantage and escape the sleek galley. Rona's first goal was to travel as far from Loch Indaal as possible. Perhaps the galley would cry off once it reached the storm-tossed waves of open water.

Making the most of the wind and waves, the *Puthaid*

raced ahead of the storm, the galley in pursuit and gaining steadily. Rona's heartbeat raced in excitement and dread.

Against hope, the galley did not pull back once it reached the open sea. Tenacious, the craft leapt through the waves, each one drawing it closer to the *Puthaid.*

"They continue to gain, despite the storm and the waves," Brant noted.

"We cannae lead them to the *Banríon Laoch,"* Rona replied. "And we cannae allow them to turn about and warn others of the direction we've taken." She included each man in her gaze. "Our sides are too high for them to board easily, and the deeper draft makes us more stable even in the storm. Our only option is to lead them out to sea."

"They will either capsize or turn and head back."

The men exchanged glances. Brant grinned. "I think I like pirating."

Lightning split the sky. The *Puthaid* rolled against a strong wave. Rona stumbled against the rail, striking her shoulder painfully. Another man spelled Brant at the rudder, fighting the waves pushing them inland. The galley took advantage of a sudden change of wind that left the Puthaid momentarily adrift and rowed west, closing in like a colley dog after a recalcitrant sheep. A hard draw on the rudder kept them from floundering too close to shore, but it brought the galley close enough for Rona to count eight determined men at the oars. The odds had just gotten steeper.

The oarsmen's efforts doubled as they closed on the *Puthaid.* Two rose, pulling their oars from the sea. The *Puthaid* rode another swell then plunged into a wave's trough, bringing them almost on level with the smaller galley. A three-pronged iron hook arced through the sky, trailing a length of rope. It struck the deck. Chips of wood sprayed through the air. With a hoarse cry, Brant grabbed an axe from a hook at the rail and, with a swift blow, hacked the rope in half. Freed, the rope whipped over the side. Another hook, falling short, struck the Puthaid's side with a thud.

"They're trying to board us!" the man at the helm shouted.

Rona raised her voice above the wind. "Can ye throw a jar from here?"

Brant set aside his axe then stepped forward, hefting the small clay pot in one hand. "Och, aye. 'Twill be like tossing apples from a tree at me cousins." He sent Rona a broad wink. "Nae that I would ever have done such a thing."

He stepped close to the rail. "Hold her steady, Blane," he admonished the man at the rudder. Rearing back, he took two quick steps forward and hurled the urn toward the galley. A wave pushed the bow of the galley up and the cask struck the prow. It burst open, flinging white powder into the air and over the sea.

Instantly, Brant was handed another. He stepped backward and lofted the cask next to his shoulder. Again, he stepped forward and, using the momentum of his motion, flung the clay vessel across the water. This time it landed square on the deck of the galley. Cries of surprise and pain filled the air as the quicklime mixed with rain and sea spray, burning skin, clothing, and eyes. Rona watched with fascinated dread as several men flung themselves overboard in an attempt to rid themselves of the quicklime. Those remaining slapped their arms, tilting their faces up to be washed in the driving rain. With a keening cry, one ripped his tunic over his head then also plunged into the icy waters.

Rona eyed the distance from the galley to the shore and the pound of waves against the rocky shore.

"They willnae make it," she said. Guilt tore at her. Her way was not death. The Black MacNeill did not kill those she encountered. Yet, her actions had sent these men to their deaths. The single MacDonnell remaining aboard would not be able to pilot the galley by himself and would be dashed upon the rocks with the ill-fated ship.

"Ye know their intent," Brant reminded her. "They carried swords at their belts and would have given no quarter for stealing the *Puthaid*. The price for letting ye escape would also likely have been their deaths."

She stared over the sea, searching for any indication the men had reached the shore. The waves did not give them up, and she at last turned away as the galley broke apart with a groan of tortured timber upon the rocks.

"Go," she commanded, sick at heart even knowing she'd done what was needed.

The *Puthaid* obeyed the command at her rudder and plunged back toward open water.

Pedr's breath came in pants as he squatted behind a large rock not far from the docks. The chill of the approaching winter storm seeped into his bones though he'd been warm enough from his exertions only moments before. The cut on his head stung.

The track to the port had been largely empty, though a body of possibly ten or more men had ridden north with haste almost half an hour earlier. Lanterns winked in the distance, swaying from hooks as the wind buffeted the shore.

"There's nae ship as will take us this night," Sten murmured as he hunkered down next to Pedr. "MacDonnell's men will have seen to that, even if the storm hadnae closed the port." He peered at the sky. "We should take shelter and see what may be done when the worst of the squall is past."

Pedr shook his head. "I dinnae like remaining here longer. They willnae expect us to cross the Sound in such weather. Surprise is on our side."

Sten snorted. "*I* wouldnae expect us to attempt a crossing this night, either. 'Tis a desperate gambit—and likely one we wouldnae survive. Nae, there is a kirk we passed a handful of minutes past where we will find refuge."

Pedr considered his uncle's council. They were all wet and cold, and though the Sound was not wide, the frenzied waves would make short work of a coracle such as they'd crossed the loch in, and no ship capable of ferrying them would do so. They were stuck, at least for a time, and a church was as good a place as any to seek shelter. After experiencing the treachery of Aonghus Og's hospitality, he doubted even holy ground would afford them much refuge.

"Aye. Only until the storm dies down. We will travel the instant 'tis possible."

Sten rose and motioned for the others to follow. They wended their way inland and stumbled upon a small kirk not too far distant. Sporadic moonlight revealed walls covered in moss and lichen, and the thatch roof in sad need of repair. One end of the building had been dismantled—possibly to harvest the stones to build a larger kirk under construction a short distance away. But the relief to be out of the wind and sheltered from the icy rain was immediate, and those not on guard duty immediately rolled in their wet plaides and fell asleep.

"Do ye think she reached the ship, Uncle?"

"Aye. 'Twas a brilliant ploy to convince Aonghus Og she's of a delicate disposition and nae threat to him—and good fortune she'd sent her uncle to sell the ships so he dinnae recognize her. She will have made it to the ship where Haldor can be trusted to sail for Morvern and help. Though we can hope to avoid battle, 'twill be nice to have the Baron's support."

Sten's confidence did not reassure Pedr. He'd just turned his wife over to the MacDonnell chief, hoping he'd keep his word and send her to Morvern. If she wasn't being held prisoner at Finlaggan and was able to deliver her message—alliances with Brant's family be damned—his da would descend upon Islay, not with ransom in hand, but with the utter wrath of God.

He pushed away from the door frame and paced the length of the nave to what must have once been the altar, careful of his footing in the gloom. A large, rather flat stone rested askew atop a wooden platform. Still uneasy, Pedr traced his fingertips over the marks carved into the top and sides of the stone. They were barely discernable to the eye, worn with centuries of such caresses. How many others had sought solace before him?

He sat on the shallow step which elevated the altar and placed his face in his hands.

I cannae risk my men's lives in this storm—but avoiding capture will become more and more difficult the longer we remain. 'Tis nae a big isle, and Aonghus Og controls every square inch of it.

The floor was little more than shadows in the gloom, but a flash of lightning through an aperture in the wall betrayed something near his boot. Curious, he pushed through the dirt and other debris until his fingers touched a round object no larger in diameter than a silver coin.

Holding it aloft, he peered at the circlet of gold. Recognizing it as a ring, he discovered it was set with a dark stone. The ring itself was covered in some form of design he could not discern other than by touch. Feeling somewhat better for the distraction, he slipped the ring inside the pouch at his belt and settled in for the duration of the storm.

Pedr's uncle shook him awake. Through the open end of the chapel, he sighted dark clouds racing across the sky, chased by the waning light of the moon. But it was a comfort to note the rain had ceased and no lightning broke the night.

"'Tis only an hour or so before dawn," Sten said. "The storm has subsided, and mayhap the MacDonnells will wait until first light to begin the search again. Let us be quick."

The rest of the MacLeans were awake, making preparations for their trek. Within a few minutes, they were ready and crept into the open, clinging to the remaining shadows as they returned to the docks.

"How are we to command passage?" Sten grumbled. "All have been warned against us, and there are too few of us to steal a ship."

"Where's a good pirate when ye need one?" Pedr quipped, feeling unaccountably better for a couple of hours' sleep. A faint chuckle from the others rewarded his question.

"We'll travel north and search for a fishing boat that survived the storm," he said. "The Sound opens up nae too far from here—a likely place to find such a boat."

They wound their way north and west, following paths through the hills—no fishing boats sighted—until they reached a small cove, the sweep of its harbor sheltering it from the east.

"We lost sight of Jura some time back," Sten noted. "I fear the trip across the Sound from here will be more dangerous."

Sten grabbed Pedr's arm. "Look!" He pointed to a dark object in the harbor.

Pedr stared—squinted his eyes. "It cannae be." He shook his head then looked again.

"'Tis the *Banríon Laoch!*"

Chapter Fourteen

Sten gripped Pedr's shoulder. "Why would she be at harbor here?"

Pedr understood his uncle's restraint. He hadn't lived as a pirate for over four decades without learning caution. But it was difficult to resist the urge to race down the hill to the ship. Why was the *Banríon Laoch* still here on Islay, but not at Port Askaig? Who commanded the ship, and where was Rona?

"I dinnae know, Uncle. Mayhap we should find out."

Sten released his grip and they hurried down the slope, slipping and sliding in the mud. Reaching the ship, Pedr approached alone, his men spread out behind him.

"Ahoy the ship!"

"Welcome to the *Banríon Laoch,* Sir Pedr!" came Haldor's familiar voice. "Come aboard."

Pedr climbed aboard, followed by the others. Blankets and mugs of heated ale were immediately offered—proof Haldor's guard had seen them as they descended the slope.

"Where's my wife?"

To Pedr's relief, Haldor did not look surprised—which meant she'd arrived and hadn't been held by Aonghus Og as prisoner—but a look of distress crossed his cousin's face which did not bode well.

"She demanded we drop her at the head of Loch Guinart."

Pedr waited to hear the rest, but it was clear he was going to have to draw the answers from Haldor one at a time. He hesitated, giving himself a moment to remove the displeasure from his voice.

"And why would my wife wish a tour of Loch Guinart when she'd been instructed to sail for Morvern?"

"'Tis close to Loch Indaal, she said."

Pedr opened his mouth for the next question, then realized he already knew the answer. She'd gone to Loch Indaal to steal the *Puthaid.*

"Shite!" He clenched his fists, aware of his heart pounding like a smithy's hammer in his chest. "Ye did naught to stop her?"

Haldor spread his hands. "I dinnae believe locking her in the cabin would have worked for long. And even though she's a pirate, placing yer new bride in restraints below decks dinnae appeal."

Pedr's glare swept from the regret on Haldor's face to the smirk twitching Sten's lips. Raging fury rose against the reality he'd not married a biddable lass. However, if anyone could steal the *Puthaid* a second time, Rona could.

"Brant and three others went with her."

His anger expelled in a harsh breath, feeling guilty he'd had no thought for his cousin.

"She was dressed as the Black MacNeill," Haldor offered.

Pedr shook his head and grinned, his ire defeated at last by the image. "Damn, but I'll bet it looked good on her." Not pausing for an answer, he bellowed, "Get this ship under weigh! We've a pirate to catch!"

Rona peered over the rail, more weary than she could remember in a long time. The storm had left them all drenched and exhausted, driving home the wisdom of avoiding storms in the Isles. Even her hardy crew had ceased their banter hours past, though they'd each caught brief naps from time to time during the night once the storm had passed. She'd been unable to sleep despite their insistence she rest. The sense of being chased as prey was too strong.

Once they left the galley behind and rounded the southern-most point of Islay, they'd been forced to seek shelter in a small bay until the worst of the storm had passed. Using the following strong winds, the *Puthaid* had quickly made up for lost time, and daybreak found them sailing up the western coast of Islay. As they approached the mouth of Loch Guinart, she spotted the silhouette of a ship's mast against the pearl-gray sky.

At her shout, Brant immediately ordered the sail trimmed and turned the ship toward shore, hoping to find a cove to hide in before they were spotted. He leapt to the rail, hand bladed over his eyes to shade them from the early rays of the sun.

"'Tis the *Banríon Laoch* or I'll give up my pirate sash this day."

"Ye're nae a pirate, laddie," another called. "Merely a wee thief."

"Wheesht! I'm sailin' with the Black MacNeill. Makes me a pirate. Makes us *all* pirates."

Rona ignored their banter, her heart in her throat. "Are ye certain 'tis the *Banríon Laoch*?"

"I've sailed on her these past two years," Brant boasted, "and can find her amid a forest o' ships even drunk as a lord and comin' back from . . .. Ow! What was that for?"

"Ye're speaking to Lady MacLean," the other man growled, "nae matter she's a pirate. Watch yer tongue."

Brant glanced at Rona and his face reddened. "My apologies, my lady. I would have been comin' back from Mass, honest truth. Ow! What?"

The older man snorted. "Drunk? At Mass?"

Brant's cheeks blushed deeper.

Rona laughed, her spirits rising higher as the other ship approached. "Heave to!"

"Aye!"

Within a few minutes, the *Banríon Laoch* drew near.

Rona stood upon the rail, one hand braced in the rigging. The wind tore strands of hair free from her black scarf to whip about her head. Even at a distance, she knew Pedr's form. He balanced easily against the roll of the ship, feet spread wide, hands clasped behind his back.

"Ahoy, *Banrion Laoch*!" she called, hand cupped to her lips.

"Ahoy, the *Puthaid*!" Came the reply. "Stand by and prepare to be boarded."

Rona was overjoyed to find Pedr alive and well and apparently suffering no lingering effects of his imprisonment beyond a small gash above one eye which would likely leave him with a scar—and give him an even more rakish appearance. She grinned and grabbed his arms, then—catching him off-guard—pulled her to him for a firm kiss. A cheer went up. Not only had they escaped the MacDonnell's clutches, but they also had the *Puthaid*—and Rona's heart-felt embrace echoed the jubilation of all on board.

A heady mixture of triumph and embarrassment warmed her. Pedr snaked his arm about her waist and drew her against his side.

"Shall we sail for home, *mo leannan*?"

"Aye. Who shall captain the *Puthaid*?"

Pedr grinned. "Who else but the Black MacNeill?"

Pedr leaned his shoulders against the wall of the cabin beneath the aftcastle, face turned into the breeze. Rona relaxed next to him, and he drew comfort from the casual touch of their arms and hips.

The coracle they'd set adrift with the MacDonnell's men disappeared in the distance.

"Och, I forgot." He opened the pouch at his belt. "I found something ye may like." He drew forth the ring and held it up to the sun's light. "'Tis much nicer than I thought, though 'twas dark when I stumbled upon it."

"'Tis lovely," Rona said. "Where did ye find it?"

"On the floor of the auld kirk, half hidden in the dirt. I suppose someone dropped it years ago. It looks verra auld."

Sten shoved away from the rail. "May I see that?"

About to hand the ring to Rona, Pedr gave her a quick smile of apology and dropped it into his uncle's hand. "What do ye know of it?"

Sten turned it over and ran his fingertip across the gold. "Nice detail. 'Tis gold bead-work on the band—probably worked with gold wire and worn smooth with age. The stone, though." He pursed his lips. After a moment's thought, he licked the pad of his thumb and stroked the surface of the stone. It glowed deep red.

"Och, 'tis chipped," Rona noted.

"Nae. 'Tis engraved." He held it out, pointing to the stone. "The garnet has a wee horse etched on it. Here—look closely."

"The horse has a fish tail!" she exclaimed.

Sten smiled. "'Tis because this is a Roman trinket. The Romans have a mythical creature call *hippocampus*—or water horse."

Rona marveled. "I've nae seen the like."

Pedr spoke up. "If I remember my history lessons—Hippocamp was the horse of Poseidon, god of the seas." He accepted the ring from his uncle and handed it to Rona. "It suits ye."

"Thank ye, Pedr." Her eyes glowed. She slipped the ring on her finger and raised her hand, turning it so the dark red stone caught the light. "I'd like to learn more about Poseidon, and the hippocampus, and . . . och, *everything*!"

"*Mo chridhe,* I am happy to share my world with ye. We will travel far and learn of it together."

"Land ho!"

Though they'd been sailing in sight of islands and the Scottish mainland for hours, Pedr knew they'd sighted the opening to Loch Aline, and that Morvern, the seat of Baron MacLean—and Pedr's home—lay just ahead.

He grinned. "We're almost home, Rona. And just in time for Yule."

Chapter Fifteen

Pedr glanced up as Alex burst through the people crowding the dock, shouting his name. His twin leapt aboard the *Puthaid* then grabbed his arm and pummeled his shoulder, a grin of excitement on his face.

"Ye wee skellum! We've been worrit, ye've been gone so long." He tilted his head. "Da's bletherin' on how ye missed two evenings with the Beath and Macilvera lasses. He expected ye to announce yer betrothal this night at the end of the Yule celebrations. Though I will say he'll be pleased to have the *Puthaid* returned." He glanced at the ship then back to his brother, a wide grin on his face. "Ye canny bastard! Ye really did it!"

Pedr returned the brotherly blow, sending Alex staggering to the side. "I've brought home more than a ship, brother. I've brought my bride."

The shock on Alex's face gave Pedr the reaction he'd hoped for. His jaw hung slack, hands useless at his sides.

"Ye what?"

"Come. I've a tale to tell ye." Pedr led Alex off to the side and gave a nod to where Rona stood speaking with Sten and Brant only a few steps away. Sunlight shone on her head, making a halo of her golden hair. She still wore her black tunic and trews, and her seal-skin cloak hung from her shoulders. Murdo's white whiskers peered from beneath the hem.

She looked deliciously dangerous.

"Who is this?" Alex asked.

"My wife." Pedr raised his voice. "Rona!"

She glanced up. Her eyes widened as her gaze slid from

him to Alex then back. Twice. She murmured something to Sten and Brant—who laughed—then crossed the planks to where Pedr and his brother stood. Pride swelled Pedr's heart. Her grace came from the rolling decks of a ship, loose-limbed and free. Her cheeks flushed with the sun and wind, and light creases fanned from the outer corners of her eyes with humor and from long hours squinting into the sun.

Clad in her pirate attire, she was striking, and Pedr was immensely pleased she was his.

She leaned close to murmur in his ear. "There are two of ye?" Her gaze cut to Alex.

Pedr chuckled. "*Mo chridhe*, may I present my brother, Alex MacLean?"

"I am pleased tae meet ye, Sir Alex," she replied with a smile. Murdo yipped warningly at Alex as he took a hesitant step forward.

"Nice dog—one of ours?"

"He's from the *Puthaid.* I've named him Murdo," Rona replied.

"Alex, my bride, Lady Rona MacNeill, now a MacLean." He gloated as his brother sought his tongue.

"The pleasure is all mine, m'lady. I look forward to hearing of yer adventures the past few days—and yer wedding to which Ma and Ama werenae invited." It was Alex's turn to gloat for Pedr knew his face had flushed at his brother's pointed reminder. Though he felt certain both women would love Rona, his omission would likely earn him a scathing rebuke.

Brant strolled over. "I was," he gloated, grinning at Alex's disbelieving look. "And ye willnae believe . . .."

"As ye can see," Pedr interrupted, turning the topic away from future trouble, "I've followed Da's demands to the letter."

Alex laughed. "'Twill take some doing to convince *him* of that. He's been a right bear grumbling over yer absence—

though 'twas clear he was worrit." He glanced at Rona, bemusement tilting the corner of his mouth. "Tell me how ye met yer bride"

"'Twas over the theft of the *Puthaid*," Pedr said. "Chief MacNeill swore he knew how to find the ship and would share his information—if Rona and I wed."

"Ye got the better of the bargain, I must say. Ye've always had the devil's own luck. Ye recovered the ship *and* found a bonnie bride?" Alex cocked his head, turning his attention to the new Lady MacLean. "What drew ye to my brother?"

"A hangman's noose," she replied. Alex stared. Brant snickered.

Pedr guffawed. Alex at a loss for words twice in one day—nae, in a mere handful of minutes—was fine, indeed.

Alex scowled. "He threatened to hang ye?"

Rona shrugged, though mischief lurked in her gray eyes. "'Twas an option."

Alex shot a horrified look between Brant and his twin.

Pedr took pity on him. "I was enchanted by Lady Rona from the moment I met her, and couldnae let her slip away. She was disinclined to agree to the wedding until I pointed out as my wife, she would be above suspicion."

"Suspicion of what?" Alex demanded.

"Of piracy."

This time Alex's gaze slid from Rona's head to her black garb, eyes widening as realization san in. "Ye're the Black MacNeill?"

"Aye. Or, I was whilst it served my purpose."

"What purpose was that, if ye dinnae mind my asking?"

"Feeding my clan."

"She's put the ship's stores to good use," Pedr said. "The MacNeills will fare better this winter than in the past, thanks to her."

Alex mulled over the information. "Ye've been gone

several days. All of it with the MacNeills?"

Pedr and Rona and Brant exchanged glances. It had been decided they would say as little as possible of her identity as the Black MacNeill and of their misadventure on Islay. Rumors—no matter how rooted in truth—tended to find their way into the wrong ears.

"This should wait until we're alone," Pedr said with a pointed look at the bustle around them.

"Ye have a cut over yer eye," Alex noted. "Da isnae going to like this, is he?"

Pedr clapped his twin on his shoulder. "Nae at all. But at least now 'tis easier to tell us apart."

Alex snorted. "I dinnae know what he's talking about, sister," he said in aside to Rona. "I've clearly always been the better-looking of the two of us."

Rona hazarded a smile around the sudden fear Pedr's words evoked. *Alone.* He meant in conference with his da, Baron MacLean. Everyone knew of the Baron. He was a huge man of Norse descent, with a temper to match his stature. She glanced at Pedr's and Alex's relaxed manner. Even Brant didn't seem dismayed over the coming discussion. Surely rumors of the baron were exaggerated.

She shook her head. She hadn't expected Pedr and Alex to look so much alike. Indeed, dressed in similar clothing, she'd be hard-pressed to tell them apart. Today, however, Pedr sported several days' growth of beard, stained and torn clothing, and a newly-healing wound over his eye, while his brother was clean-shaven and clad in a well-wrought cloak over a tunic dyed an eye-catching blue. It wasn't so difficult to determine one from the other, though their similarities were striking. Rona couldn't help but steal another assessing look at the brothers—who looked nothing at all like their cousin Brant. Or Sten or Haldor, for that matter.

Her musings came to a chilling halt as she considered

her own attire, reminded of her humble origins and less-than-ladylike demeanor. Would his family see her as an unsuitable choice of wife for their son—the son of a baron? Would they think it possible she married Pedr only for wealth and position?

Her sealskin cloak was weather-proof and warm. But it appeared shabby compared to Alex's heavy woolen one woven in a dark green and black plaid. Her black tunic and leggings fit her well, and the heavy leather belt with the wrought silver buckle would have cost a fortune—had she not pulled it from a chest in one of the English vessels she'd stolen the year before. But it was not a lady's garb.

What would they make of her?

She startled at Pedr's light tug on her hand.

"Sten and Haldor will see to the ship. Shall we head to the castle?"

Brant saluted with a jaunty grin. "As much as I'd like to hide in a corner and observe the meeting ahead, I'm nae likely to be missed, and also have duties aboard ship." He nudged Alex. "Meet with me over a mug of whisky before supper?"

With Alex's agreement, the three of them disembarked and moved beyond the docks.

Alex nodded. "I had horses brought for ye when I heard ye'd arrived," he informed his brother. "Lady Rona may ride mine."

"She'll ride with me," Pedr retorted.

Rona glanced up in apprehension. She'd never been closer to a horse than those in stables near the docks she frequented . . . used to frequent.

Pedr accepted the reins of a tall red horse whose coat gleamed in the sun then swung into the saddle as Alex tossed a coin to the lad attending the horses. He reached a hand toward Rona and kicked his left foot from the stirrup. "Mount up behind me."

She eyed his hand then the tall horse. How on earth would she climb atop the leggy beast?

"Caith is a gentleman," Pedr said in a gentle voice that took notice of her apprehension. "Nae harm will come to ye. Place yer foot in the stirrup and use my hand to swing up."

Alex stepped closer, offering safety should she slip. Swallowing her trepidation, she did as Pedr directed, wincing only slightly as she straddled the beast's back. She settled firmly against Pedr, arms about his waist. The dip and sway of the horse as he accustomed himself to her weight was a similar sensation to being aboard a ship. It wasn't so bad after all.

They set off through the village, Murdo yipping happily at the horses' heels, and soon MacLean Castle came into view. Rona tightened her grip.

"Dinnae fash, *mo leannan.* They will love ye."

That remained to be seen. Her fingers loosened. "'Tis a big castle."

Pedr chuckled. "Aye. But 'tis my home, and now yers."

That was not a foregone conclusion in her mind, either. Panic rose as they rode through the gates. Would the baron and baroness deem her unworthy and insist their marriage be annulled?

"There are more people in the bailey than in my entire clan," Rona whispered.

"None as bonnie as ye," he replied. His sweet words didn't help.

He reined Caith to a halt then handed Rona down. She eyed the massive double doors framed by round towers and hung with evergreen wreaths twined with branches bearing red berries. Pretty and festive, but behind the Yule decorations, her future awaited.

"Welcome to MacLean Castle, my love," he said. The doors to the hall opened, and they strode inside.

Warmth and the scent of candles and burning peat

greeted her. Fresh-cut evergreens, lavender and fennel in the rushes, and the ever-present odor of bodies mixed with the tang of newly-dyed cloth added to the aroma. She halted, unable to make her feet carry her one step farther into the enormous room. Murdo sat next to her with a whine.

A tall, slender woman, with Pedr's dark hair and eyes bustled across the room, arms out-stretched in greeting. Her glance landed on Rona and her step slowed.

"Welcome," she said, her hands falling to her waist as her gaze traveled from Rona to Pedr and back.

A bear of a man, dark hair liberally sprinkled with gray, stepped behind the woman, a scowl on his face.

"Good to have ye home, son. I hear ye brought the *Puthaid* home," he rumbled.

The woman laid a hand on his forearm. "He also brought home a guest," she admonished him, her voice calm but firm.

The man's gaze cut to Rona and his bushy brows lifted. "My apologies. Ye are . . .?"

"I will apologize for my husband," the woman said. "His worry has made him abrupt. Since my son has either left his manners at the dock or is in trepidation of rousing his da's ire, I will introduce myself. I am Carys Wen MacLean," the woman said. "This is my husband, Birk, Baron MacLean."

Rona's breath caught to find herself before one of the most powerful men in Western Scotland. He was as legend portrayed him—towering above all present except his sons who shared his height, firm of muscle, and a commanding presence. He wasn't likely to think kindly of a poor MacNeill lass marrying his son, chief's daughter or not. Rona swallowed her unease and lifted her chin.

Pedr twitched as if he'd been nudged. "Mother, Father, may I introduce Rona MacNeill, now MacLean—my wife."

In the sudden silence, Rona heard the faint rustle of feet on the rushes as Murdo shifted his weight to lean against her leg. Lady MacLean's expression of surprise paled in comparison to the thunderous narrow-eyed look of suspicion the baron leveled on Pedr.

Lady MacLean recovered quickly and managed a warm smiled. "Welcome to MacLean Castle, Rona. Shall we take refreshment in the solar?" She leveled her question at them all, punctuated by a sharp tug on Baron MacLean's arm. With a short nod, he allowed himself to be led away, and Rona, Pedr, and Alex followed. Lady MacLean paused and spoke to a woman. "Aine, please find Hanna and ask her to join us."

"I wouldnae miss this for all the gold in Persia," Alex chuckled. "Da's going to have to swallow a lot of words he willnae say before Ma."

Pedr elbowed his brother. Rona struggled to breathe.

The lord's solar held shelves along an entire wall, filled with books and rolled parchments. Chief MacNeill's solar held few books—none of which she could read—and parchment was all but unheard of. The bit her wedding contract had been written on had seen much previous use.

Pots and statues and tiny chests, no doubt from far-away places Rona had never heard of, fought for space on the shelves and in nooks along the wall. Never had she seen such casual extravagance. The shapes and colors and intricate carvings set her mind awhirl, and her heart raced to recall Pedr's promise to explore the world. Her hands itched to hold the lovely baubles, but she forced her attention to the matter at hand.

Lady MacLean took a seat, motioning for Rona to do the same. She settled on the edge of a cushioned chair, feeling the need to position herself to flee if necessary. The others scattered themselves about the room, Baron MacLean in his seat behind the heavy, cluttered desk. Pedr leaned a hip on the arm of Rona's chair.

The door opened and a tall, thin, older woman, her once-blonde hair now faded to a mere glitter of gold amongst silver, stepped inside the room. Her gaze fell immediately to Rona. Alex and Pedr settled her into a comfortable chair.

Lady MacLean made the introductions. "My mother by marriage, Hanna MacLean."

"I am verra pleased tae meet ye," Rona replied.

Hanna's eyes slid from Rona's worn boots to her bare head. "She's naught like the dainty lasses my son has paraded about the hall this past sennight. She wears sensible clothing and those hands of hers have seen more toil than plying an embroidery needle." Her gaze cut to Pedr. "She's pretty, too. I hope ye've wed her."

Rona blinked. This was the formidable baron's mother. *She doesnae know me, yet she already approves?* A bit of her confidence returned. She glanced at Pedr, warming beneath his smile.

"Oh, he did," Carys assured the older woman. "Without saying a word to either of us."

Hanna cackled, her eyes filled with humor. "An apple doesnae fall far from the tree, eh, Birk?"

"Now that we are only family here, Pedr," Lady MacLean continued, "please tell us how ye met Rona."

Pedr glanced from his ma to his da and placed a hand on Rona's shoulder. "I'd gone to the Isle of Gigha to speak with Laird MacNeill about the ship. Rona is his daughter." He sent a sidelong look to his ama.

"That's all?" Baron MacLean thundered as it became clear Pedr had finished his statement.

"Och, I believe there's a wee bit more to it than that," Alex drawled.

Pedr shifted slightly on the chair arm, his palm slid possessively across Rona's shoulders. "'Tis enough. We will make a fine life together, she and I."

Lady MacLean turned a kind smile on Rona. "Is this the way of it, *enaid*?"

Pedr leaned close to Rona. "She likes ye," he noted.

"'Tis a term of endearment."

"Of course, I like her," his ma retorted. "Why should I not? She has eyes only for ye and has clearly won yer heart."

"The MacNeills arenae our allies," Baron MacLean grumbled.

"Och, they are now," Pedr replied amiably. "In fact, I wouldnae be surprised if the MacDonnell doesnae trade with them again."

Birk slapped his hands on the desk, the sound startling Rona—and everyone else except Lady MacLean and Hanna. "Did MacDonnell have my ship?"

"Er, aye . . .." Pedr cut a glance to his ma.

Rona's pulse quickened as the tension in the room rose.

"There's surely more to the story," Lady MacLean asserted.

"Did Aonghus Og steal the *Puthaid*?" the baron demanded.

Rona's hands clenched in her lap. Whether it meant her imprisonment or even death, she could not sit back and allow war to brew between the two clans.

"Nae," she said. "I did."

Chapter Sixteen

Baron MacLean rose from his seat to lean over his desk, his glare fixed on Rona. "Ye are a lass. Ye cannae . . .."

Hanna interrupted. "Have ye learned naught of women, Birk MacLean? Sit. Stop intimidating the girl. Let her speak."

Drawing courage from the older woman's apparent support, Rona continued.

"I—and a few in my clan—have stolen several *English* ships the past few years," she said, stressing the word *English*. "'Twas a verra foggy night when we chose your ship in Maryport. We dinnae expect a Scottish cog to be harbored amongst the English ladies."

Baron MacLean's eyebrows slid together above his nose. "Ye're saying, if ye'd known 'twas my ship, ye'd have nae taken it?"

Rona twisted her mouth to the side then shook her head. Lying might ease his temper, but it would not serve. "Nae. I'm saying I dinnae intentionally look for a Scottish ship. I heard the sheep in the hold and knew 'twas the ship I needed to see my people through the winter. When I realized 'twas the *Puthaid*—and nae Englishman would give his ship such a name—I couldnae turn back."

Birk drew a breath, then rounded on Rona. "Couldnae or wouldnae?"

"Both. We were too far from port to return before dawn in a dense fog. Nor did I wish to give up our night's work. Her cargo alone was worth the risk. Ridding ourselves of the ship was a different matter. 'Tis how Aonghus Og came to have possession."

Birk sank back into his chair, splitting his gaze between

his sons before aiming a finger at Pedr. "I thought ye said ye suspected the Black MacNeill was behind the theft of the ship."

"Och, 'tis true enough," Alex agreed, a sly grin spreading across his face.

Pedr kicked the leg of his brother's chair.

Birk rubbed his chin. "Well, I'm glad ye found the ship even if the pirate wasnae involved. He should be hanged for the trouble he's caused."

"Och, I wouldnae go so far," Pedr cautioned.

"What? Why?" his da demanded. "Hanging's too good for him. I'll nae have my shipping disrupted by the likes of another pirate."

"Uncle Sten and Haldor were once pirates," Alex needled.

"They've reformed," Birk corrected, a warning in his voice.

Rona's heart threaded a rapid beat. She fought the urge to flee the room—and ultimately the hangman's noose. She sought Pedr's eyes and found him . . . laughing.

"What's so funny?" Birk demanded.

"Da, Rona is the Black MacNeill."

His da's eyebrows shot upward and an *oof* of surprise escaped him. After a moment he relaxed, and a slow grin creased his face.

"'Tis nae often I am surprised." He drew his gaze over her garb. "Clothing of a woman used to a ship's deck. Hands roughened by ropes and sea water." He cast a sidelong glance to his wife. "She should fit right in."

"She will," Pedr claimed. "And for more reasons than this."

Birk raised a thick brow. "Aye?"

"Aye. She agreed to marry me and avoid the noose."

The baron scowled.

Carys laughed out loud. "Ye cannae cry foul, my love,

for it resembles the marriage proposal I received twenty or so years ago."

Baron MacLean's face reddened. Rona worried he might succumb to a heart seizure.

Hanna cackled and slapped her knee. "Young Pedr is just like his da. I've always said so."

Birk ran a hand over his head. "Shite! Can the two of ye nae forget that tale?"

"Of course not," Carys said, but her voice said the memory was much less painful to her than it appeared to be to her husband. "It seems Pedr *does* listen from time to time."

"I got the idea from ye, Da," Pedr claimed. "I couldnae let the opportunity pass. She is exactly what I need—a partner who loves the sea as much as I do. We've plans to travel the world together."

"As ye should," Carys said. She rose to her feet. "Howbeit, the poor child must be exhausted." She beckoned to Rona. "Come. Bring yer wee dog. Hanna and I will see to yer comfort." She cast a glare and pointed finger at her son. "Pedr, ye will be notified when she has rested. Dinnae think ye've escaped the consequences of marrying without yer family knowing."

Not entirely certain if she'd passed the baron's approval—and much in awe of the two older MacLean ladies, Rona cast a look at Pedr. He stood and she accepted his offered hand as she rose. A twinkle in his eyes, he raised her fingers to his lips and kissed them lightly.

"Go. Ye are safe, though they'll likely pester ye with a thousand questions."

"'Tisnae an interrogation, Pedr," Carys chided.

"Gossip. Nae more," Hanna nodded.

Reluctantly, Rona turned to go. Pedr's hand tightened on hers and he pulled her back, catching both of her hands to his chest as he touched his forehead to hers. "I will be up soon.

Dinnae fash." He pressed a kiss to her temple then stepped away, releasing her hands.

With a smile on her lips and a lighter heart, Rona and Murdo followed Carys and Hanna from the room.

They climbed stone steps to the third floor where the family lived. Rona tried hard to keep her mouth closed as she entered a tower room with windows on three sides and a merry fire crackling in a brazier in the middle of the room. Sumptuously stuffed chairs sat near the windows, and heavy tapestries not only hung on the wall, but graced the floor as well.

Rona hesitated, but Carys and Hanna trod the costly carpets without pause.

"Aine is having a bath brought here—I thought it cozier than either bedroom, and Pedr will not likely check here first," Carys confided.

"'Tis a woman's retreat," Hanna replied. She sank into a chair with a sigh. "My auld bones prefer these cushions."

As several lads hefted steaming buckets of water and dumped them into a tub big enough to float a ship—or at least a small coracle—Rona eyed the two women. They couldn't have been more different, yet she sensed a close, affectionate bond between the pair. Carys, tall and lithe, her dark hair and eyes a distinct contrast to the older woman's silvered blonde hair.

The lads finally finished their task and closed the door to the solar behind them as they quit the room. Carys helped Rona doff her gear and settle amid the bone-aching heat of the tub.

"She's just what we hoped for our Pedr, eh, Carys?"

Rona glanced up, startled by the older woman's statement. "What do ye mean?"

"Dinnae mind Hanna," Carys soothed. "At her age, she's given herself permission to say exactly what she thinks. She's right, though. We knew Pedr wouldnae be happy with any of the lasses his da has invited over the past sennight."

"Pah!" Hanna waved a hand. "Dainty lasses arenae for the likes of our Pedr. Alex—he's destined for the barony, and he needs a woman who is bonnie enough to turn heads and content to see to the running of this pile of rocks." Hanna gave a short nod. "Pedr is different."

"He has grown up on yer tales," Carys said fondly. "Tales of bold Norse women—such as yerself—and the stories passed down of his great-great aunt Arbela who once bested a shipload of pirates off the coast of Gibraltar."

"I dinnae understand," Rona said, willing to overlook Carys' statement about the pirates. "I'm nae the sort of woman who should marry a baron's son."

"Then why did ye?" Hanna wanted to know.

Rona shrugged. "He insisted." She smiled. "And I'm glad."

"We dinnae care about yer clothing or who yer sire is," Carys said. "Hanna and I recognized a kindred spirit when we first laid eyes on ye. Bold, daring, honorable."

"Ye'll fit in, dinnae fear." Hanna nodded. "Just like I did. And his ma."

"Hanna and I—and Pedr's great-great aunt Arbela—have unusual backgrounds. Arbela and her brother—Pedr's grandfather—are half Scots, half Armenian. Ask Pedr to tell ye the tales sometime. Or, if ye're in the hall much, ye're certain to hear the stories now and again after supper. They're quite popular and are oft repeated."

A sense of belonging settled on Rona. She couldn't wait to hear the tales before the hearth. She settled deeper into the tub, content to discover she'd married into a family with kind, generous, and fierce women as unconventional as she.

* * *

Pedr waited until the door closed behind the women

before he took his seat. He was very much aware of his da's gaze fixed on him, and he was not as care-free as he'd have Rona believe.

He glanced up, as much innocence as he could muster on his face. He'd be willing to bet it fell short of his intention.

Birk leaned back in his chair, his slow, controlled movements reminding Pedr of a predator locked onto its prey. He tried a smile.

Alex cleared his throat and sent Pedr a twitch of his lips telling him not to grimace.

Birk tapped a finger on his desk. "I'd like to hear the complete story, Pedr. I knew ye'd find a way to dodge our agreement and miss the meals yer ma and I went to a great deal of trouble to arrange, but this . . .." He stabbed a forefinger at the desk. "Ye have caused yer ma a gey wheen of worry."

"I will apologize to Ma later, but it couldnae be helped." He sighed. "I was resigned—nae happy, but resigned—to the arrangement, but then I met Rona." His grin this time was real. "I couldnae help but realize I'd found the right woman for me."

"She's the Black MacNeill in truth?" Birk shook his head.

"Aye, though had she nae stolen the *Puthaid* a *second* time, I wouldnae be here to tell the tale."

"A second time?" The baron's eyebrows snapped together. "What second time?"

Pedr braced himself for the wrath certain to come.

"Her clan sold the ship to the MacDonnell—who was interested in owning a MacLean ship, and apparently has bought other ships they've taken from the English in the past. Rona's uncle admitted he'd received coin for the *Puthaid* and we sailed to Islay to get it back."

Birk's face paled. "Ye what? Damn it, Pedr, ye could

have been taken captive! We arenae openly feuding, but we arenae aligned." He glared at Pedr. "Yer Aunt Gillian wouldnae have forgiven me."

Pedr cast a look at his brother. "Er, we *were* captured."

A muscle at the corner of his da's eye twitched but he said naught. Pedr wasn't certain if that was a good sign or not.

"Only Rona, Sten, myself and three men went ashore to speak with the MacDonnell. I left Brant and Haldor in charge of the *Banríon Laoch*. The price Aonghus Og wanted for the ship was far in excess of what I had, so he arranged for us to, er, remain with him whilst he negotiated with ye. I managed to convince Aonghus Og to send Rona home with the request for coin."

Blood rushed back to Birk's face. His hands fisted on the table. "I'll kill him."

Pedr shook his head. "We escaped to be certain ye wouldnae do something ill-advised. He held me and the others for ransom, but we stole his ship."

"*My* ship!" Birk roared. "*My* son!"

"We could argue this for generations to come, Da. I dinnae know if Aonghus Og will claim foul, but if he does, 'twill be known he violated the laws of hospitality, for we ate at his table at his request, stepped into his hall, and after, were trapped."

Birk shook his head. "I dinnae like this."

"I offered to pay for the ship, Da, but he asked more than I possessed."

"We will hold a council," Birk finally said. "In the meantime, I will send ye as captain of yer own ship to ply the shipping routes from here to Lebanon."

Pedr grinned. "Rona will like that."

"Aye," the baron grumbled, "and remove two troublemakers from the area with one decision." He rubbed his chin. "In fact, 'twill be a good trip for yer cousin as well."

It was a better result than Pedr could have asked for.

Chapter Seventeen

Near Batroun, Lebanon
Mediterranean Sea
October 1301 (nine months later)

The blue-green waters of the Mediterranean slapped gently at the sides of the *Dùdach Mara* as it sailed toward the distant horizon. A blustery Sirocco de Levante wind blowing across the coastal mountains of Greece pushed their ship east toward the coast of Lebanon. Rona leaned against the rail, hair blowing about her face. Pedr smiled indulgently. His wife charmed everyone she met and had eagerly set out to learn all she could about the countries and customs they encountered along their journey. They'd lingered in each port, exploring cathedrals and gardens, inns and markets.

Her black pirate garb had been exchanged for woolens, silks, and brocades, in both fine feminine fashions and more manly garb better suited for life aboard ship. Currently, her long tunic fell to her thighs, disguising her rounded belly carrying their first child.

Rona faced him, her cheeks red from the sun and wind, eyes sparkling with excitement. "Yer son is verra active this day." She pressed a palm to her side.

He crossed the deck and placed his hand next to hers. The bairn kicked vigorously. He grinned. "My daughter is a fighter—like her ma."

"Do ye truly wish a daughter?"

"I truly wish ye both safe in my arms."

Rona squinted her eyes. "Another two months, I should think."

Pedr pressed a kiss to the side of her neck. "I can wait."

She tilted her head to the side and sighed happily. "When will we make port?"

"In a few hours," he reminded her, his mind on her hair tickling his nose and the scent of roses rising from her skin.

Rona drew his face to hers and placed a kiss on his lips. "Follow me."

With the tang of salt in the air and swaying boards beneath his feet, Pedr followed his pirate bride into their cabin. Her brocade tunic slipped over her head in a sultry dance of silvered threads and slender arms. The shortened chemise she'd adopted beneath her tunics lay fine as cobwebs over her breasts.

Pedr placed his palms on either side of her belly in a gesture of reverence. "I dinnae wish to harm the bairn."

Rona laughed. "Ye willnae." She raised a brow, exposing a twinkle in her eyes. "Dinnae deny us pleasure in these last few weeks."

He expelled a breath. "I hoped ye'd say that." His hands slid up her sides, lingering to cup her breasts. "Ye change every time I touch ye. 'Tis a marvel."

"I havenae gotten too fat?" A burr of uncertainty marred her voice.

"Never." He lowered his mouth to hers. "Let me show ye."

* * *

Tall masts lined the sky. Ships creaked at anchor as the late autumn winds rocked the waves. Gulls cried overhead. Rona swallowed hard as her morning meal rumbled irritably in her belly.

"Are ye unwell?" Pedr's observant gaze swept over her, brow crinkled with worry. "Ye appear pale. Quiet."

She shook her head. "I've weathered storms in places

whose names I cannae pronounce, but this bit of tossing doesnae agree with me this morn."

"We will be ashore soon. Do ye wish to wait in the cabin?"

"Nae. I need the open air, nae the four walls I'll be glad to see the end of."

"It has been a long voyage, *mo chroi*. And ye carrying a bairn for most of it. We will winter here then see where our journeys take us come spring."

"I think that may be a good thing." She placed a hand protectively over her belly. "Our bairn will be born in this place."

"The first MacLean born here since my great-grandda and his sister."

"It seems unreal—fantastic. I never thought to leave Scotland and the Isles, yet here I am, traveling the world." She lifted her face to Pedr. "I love our life together."

Her husband grinned. "I do, as well, *mo chroi*. I cannot wait for ye to meet the people of Batroun. Cyrus is loyal to the MacLean family and grants us rooms in a small but sumptuous guest house within his walls."

"It must be odd returning to a land where ye once held a title."

"I never did, and wouldnae wish it. My life is the sea."

He paused, fingering a length of her hair which had blown free in the breeze. "MacLean Shipping is known to be honest and without political affiliation. We pay large sums to afford the freedom to dock in Batroun—which is currently safer than Tripoli or Beirut—and our friendships go back several generations. Howbeit, we willnae leave Cyrus's grounds except with an armed guard, and ye, my love, willnae leave at all."

Rona's eyebrows lifted and a ripple of apprehension slid through her. Pedr had told her the tales of the Crusades and the fall of Acre—and of the prince of Tripoli who escaped to

Scotland many years ago and whose grandchildren still lived on the Ardnamurchan Peninsula. But to not leave the grounds? Unseen walls closed in. "I'm nae certain I will like that."

"Ye willnae remark the lack," he assured her. "Cyrus's house is quite large and his feasts are extravagant. We will, howbeit, need to leave Murdo with Brant on the ship."

"Why?"

"Cyrus's house is known as *Bayt Alqatat* which means House of the Cat." Pedr grinned. "Cyrus has quite a few of the wee beasts and I dinnae think Murdo likes cats."

Rona laughed. "Nae. He doesnae."

"Cats are revered by many here. Though Cyrus and his family are Coptic Christian, nae Muslim, 'twould ruin our visit if he chased our host's cats."

"I see. But I still dinnae think I like being bound to the house."

He eyed her rounded form. "'Tis time ye slowed a bit, mayhap?"

Rona's heart fluttered with anticipation—and a bit of dread. What would it be like to birth a bairn in a place with foreign customs? Were there superstitions she would find strange? Frightening? Blasphemous? Would they have a drink similar to the stewed Rowan berries to ward off faeries? Or a bit of rosemary to keep faeries from stealing the infant? Were the wee folk a danger to new bairns here? Would there be something more sinister?

She gave up her questions, though her stomach continued to swirl with uneasy anticipation. She had no one to talk to aboard ship about her concerns and wasn't certain she'd find it easy to confide in strange women at *Bayt Alqatat*

.

Pedr nudged her. "Look. Batroun."

Sunlight touched the buildings near the wharf, all

quarried from the same golden stone. The brilliant blue sky could not begin to compete with the turquoise waters rippling toward the shore. Dhows with colorful sails crowded the docks, and the unintelligible chatter of different languages reached Rona's ears.

"Brant has sent a messenger to Cyrus," Pedr continued, "though I daresay someone's already noted our ship and made the journey. By the time we're able to disembark, a litter and horses will be waiting to take us to the house."

"I think I'd like a bath," Rona sighed. "In a tub. Hot water." She drew a languid breath. "Lavender oil."

"Mayhap I should give Cyrus our regrets for dinner tonight? Might a feast be too much so soon?"

Rona shook her head. "Nae. I'll take a wee nap and be right as rain by supper." She sent him a fond smile. "I willnae stay up into the wee hours talking over old times, howbeit. The bairn and I need a good night's sleep."

The ship glided past vessels of every size and shape and at last bumped gently against the woven fenders lining the stone quay. Anticipation thrummed through Rona. Other ports had been exciting, but to at last see where her husband's grandfather had been born made her eager to dock.

As Pedr promised, they were met at the dock by a showing of men in luxuriously embroidered tunics. An armed guard bristling with unusual, curved swords and gleaming polearms ranged behind them, causing the flow of pedestrians to swirl behind them.

An older man stepped forward. "*Marhaba, Sidi*. I am glad to see ye."

Pedr touched his fingertips to his chest. "*Marhaban bik*, my friend. Thank ye for coming all this way. May I introduce my wife?" He turned to Rona. "*A leannan*, this is Cyrus. His family has been friends of ours for generations."

"I am pleased to meet ye," she murmured with a smile.

"*Sabah al-khayr*, my lady. I am honored to welcome ye to Batroun."

"*Sabah an-noor*," Rona replied, remembering the words Pedr had taught her.

With a wave of a hand, Cyrus brought a litter forward, carried upon the shoulders of four strong men, its white silk curtains wafting in a slight breeze.

Rona's gaze slid to Pedr. He gave a slight nod then assisted her inside the litter. She settled cautiously upon the plump cushions, startled to find a young woman seated across from her. She smiled. "*Marhaba, Sitt*. I am Dhespina."

Rona returned the greeting. "*Marhaban biki*. I am Rona."

The woman laughed. Small gold coins on her headdress tinkled merrily. "Welcome to Batroun. Cyrus is my father. His grandfather Amhal was steward when the first Baron MacLean resided here. We will be great friends."

The litter lurched as the men stepped in unison to begin the journey to Rona's new home. Dhespina lounged on her cushions.

"Relax." She reached to one side and drew forth a flask which she offered to Rona. "Drink. Ye must have a care for the babe."

A smile touched Rona's lips. She accepted the flask and drank deep of a rich, cool fruit juice.

"Thank ye. 'Twas just what I needed." She twitched a silk curtain aside. Noise and exotic aromas assailed her. From her lofty perch it seemed as if she'd exchanged a ship surrounded by water for a conveyance navigating a sea of people of all sizes, shapes, and colors. She couldn't wait to see what awaited her at the House of Cats.

Chapter Eighteen

Bayt al'asdiqa', the guest house, nestled among a copse of trees several yards distant from *Bayt Alqatat*. Rona and Pedr followed the carefully swept path between the buildings and approached the sandstone building with sweeping arches which would be their home for the next several weeks.

A large dog bounded toward them, a slight bobble to his gait. His thick, light tan coat blended well with the surroundings. A black mask surrounded his dark brown eyes and broad muzzle.

"I thought ye said Cyrus kept cats," Rona whispered.

"He does." Pedr halted as the dog sniffed his boots. With a wag of his plumed tail which curled tight at the end, the dog nudged Pedr's hand.

"This is Mushegh," Cyrus said, a fond smile on his face. "He was born with a crooked paw and thus could not keep up with the sheep he would normally herd, nor fight wolves as his kind are capable of doing."

"How does he fare with the cats?" Pedr asked.

"Rather well, actually," Cyrus replied with a chuckle. "They seem to dote on him and have been known to bring him small treats. He's spoiled, I'm afraid."

The stocky dog moved from Pedr to Rona, shoving his thick head beneath her hand, demanding his ears be scratched. She laughed.

"I like him. May he stay with us?"

Cyrus shrugged. "He has the run of the place. Since I know ye are amenable, I will not ban him from *Bayt al'asdiqa'*."

A balcony stretched across the front above the first level, shading the entry to the guest quarters. Protected by wide, iron-studded gates, the entrance led to a large interior courtyard. Numerous pots of red and pink flowers lent the courtyard a festive air. Sprawling shrubs of lavender and rosemary, and taller bay laurel trees filled the air with pungent aromas. Sunlight soaked the ground. Bright cushions were strewn beneath potted lemon trees and a peculiar tree with both red and yellow berries.

The main hall lay in the center at the rear of the house, with men's and women's quarters on either side.

"I willnae sleep so far from ye," Rona muttered after directions were given. She gripped Pedr's hand.

"We are the only guests, *mo chroi*," he said reassuringly, "and may sleep in the garden should we wish. Howbeit, the servants will keep separate quarters and ye will find bathing chambers and such with the women. Dinnae fash. They are used to our ways."

Mollified, Rona submitted to Dhespina's entreaty to follow her to the *zenana* where a bath awaited. Mushegh padded along at Rona's side with only a slight limp. A young woman, much of an age with Dhespina and Rona, met them at the entrance to a chamber on the first floor.

"This is Soraya," Dhespina said. "She will care for ye. If there is anything ye wish, ye have only to ask."

The woman bowed her head, her black hair gleaming in the light of many candles. "I am honored, *Sitt*."

Rona did not say she'd done fine on her own without a maid for more than twenty years. Things were different now, and she knew there were likely many surprises to come.

"I thank ye," she said. "I am verra tired. Might I see about that bath?"

Soraya ushered her into a large room, where a sunken tub occupied much of the space, surrounded by pierced sandstone walls which allowed the last of the summer air into the room, aromatic with scents from plants both inside and in the garden beyond. Colorful mosaic tiles covered the walls, and thick rugs lay on the floor.

Rona dropped her clothes beside the tub then stepped thankfully into the steaming water.

Mushegh leaned over the edge of the pool and whined.

"He fears for ye," Soraya said.

The dog paced the length of the pool and back. With a decisive bark, he launched himself into the water. Droplets flew high. Soraya and Dhespina shrieked as the water cascaded over their heads. Rona laughed. Mushegh paddled hard, head sliding across the top of the water.

Rona grabbed the dog's thick ruff then towed him toward the shallow end of the pool. With a shove, she boosted him out of the water. "I like ye, but I dinnae care to share my bath with ye."

Mushegh climbed from the pool and strolled toward the two women who did their best to wipe their clothing dry. Dhespina glanced at the dripping dog.

"Oh, no ye don't!" She sped to the other side of the pool, Soraya beside her.

Mushegh sighed then lowered his head and shook his coat free of water as the two women ducked out of range of the flying drops.

"I dinnae know he would jump in," Rona said as she lounged against the edge of the pool.

"He was naughty," Dhespina agreed. "At least the cats do not make such a mess."

"The cats swim?" Rona's jaw dropped, astounded.

"Yes. At least, the patriarch, Jayik, does. He seems to like it. I've seen Yasmina in the water as well, though not often."

Rona shook her head. "I think I will enjoy meeting yer cats."

Pedr took a moment to approve his rooms in the guest

house, then returned to *Bayt Alqatat* where Cyrus awaited. The lean, bearded man gestured to a plump cushion next to a low table.

"Sit. We will have refreshments and speak. I trust your rooms met with your approval?"

"Yer house is known for its generous hospitality," Pedr replied as he sank onto the cushion. He plucked a date from a small platter and popped it in his mouth. A moment later, he spat the seed into his hand.

A small white cat dropped silently from an alcove in the wall and stared up at Pedr, her round face dominated by one blue and one green eye. He gently stroked her head. Her coat slid through his fingers like the costliest silk threads.

"Still raising yer pretty cats, eh?"

"That one is Yasmina. She is quite young, and, I fear, rather deaf. At least, she chooses to only react to loud noises, and her meows are quite noticeable—as if she cannot hear herself."

"Poor lass," Pedr remarked.

"It has been noted that cats with blue eyes often show a lack of hearing," Cyrus said. "She has one green eye, and therefore perhaps does notice some sounds. Yasmina is quite safe here and should live a long life despite her partial deafness."

A young servant poured a clear liquid into a tall glass one-third full, then added water. The liquids swirled together then turned white. With a short bow, he handed the glass to Pedr who lifted the glass and sniffed. The scent of anise rose to his nose. He took a sip of the raki and felt the warmth of it slide down his throat. He took another sip then set the glass on the table. Yasmina stretched upward, placing her front paws on the edge of the table. She sniffed the glass. Pedr waved her away.

"My father sends his heartiest greetings, Cyrus."

"I know this," Cyrus replied. "His letter reached me a

sennight before your ship docked in the harbor. He told me ye and your wife have a colorful history together." He arched a brow. "There was mention of a pirate?"

Pedr laughed. "Da doesnae hide things from ye, does he?"

"No. Our families, despite the times we now live in, have ever been close."

Pedr nodded. "We had a ship go missing just before Yule and I found it had passed through the hands of a pirate. A lovely, golden-haired pirate who previously had stolen a few English ships to help feed her clan. I assure ye, she is mostly reformed."

Cyrus chuckled. "I would love to hear the story someday. For now, I am pleased to note she is soon to deliver your first child. It will be our honor to ensure she has the very best care."

"I thank ye, my friend. This lifts the care from my heart." Pedr glanced over the *mezes* on his table and chose a handful of olives from among the varied appetizers to munch on. The salty flavor balanced the sweet anise liqueur.

"Tell me how things are in Batroun. How may my family help yours?"

Cyrus set his drink aside, his mood somber. "Our city, our people, are, as always, desirous of the goods the MacLean ships bring. It burdens me to tell ye, however, time may soon come that ye will find it safer not to ply these trade routes—at least for a time. There is much strife, and it grows with each year. Ye know Lebanon fell to the Mongols more than fifty years ago. Ye may not realize that once their Khan died and much of the army withdrew, Mamluks from the south took every opportunity to gain lands in this region. Their presence—and rule—have destabilized trade and disrupted the peace of the city."

"We took care to sail north of the Barbary coast on our way here, though that is scarcely new," Pedr replied.

"'Tis not only the southern coast of the Mediterranean which troubles me. I keep in touch with those we have traded with in the past, as ye well know. One in particular ye will recall; Mihal Maldes."

Pedr nodded. The story was one he'd learned long ago. "His grandfather saved mine on two occasions whilst on Crusade. The MacLeans owe them a great debt."

Cyrus chuckled. "He claims only one such incident, though I heard the tale as ye did. Mihal's father visited here a time or two when I was a small boy, his son with him. It troubles me I have had no contact with Mihal for some months. And not only for the loss of trade. The porcelain his ships brought was exquisite, and the blue dyes are some we have difficulty getting here."

"He lives in Constantinople, aye?"

"Yes."

"'Tis nearly a thousand miles north of here."

"I would not ask ye to undertake such a journey. I merely point out how much has changed—and not for the better."

"I understand. If I thought there was something we could do, 'twould make a difference."

Cyrus nodded. "Christians are greatly disliked in this region, and the animosity between Roman Catholic and the Eastern Church is growing, which is even more troubling. My house, because of the family's standing in the city, are largely left alone, though our gates remain locked."

"Mayhap Mihal's family is merely waiting out the current rebellion."

"Mayhap. We can do little more from here. We are currently under Mamluk rule, though there are those who protest mightily."

Pedr digested the disturbing news. "We shall trouble ye only long enough for my wife to safely deliver, then be on our way."

“Do not worry yourself on our account,” Cyrus said. “Ye will be safe within our walls. Batroun is somewhat less embroiled in the rebellion than other places.”

“I thank ye. I will let my father know how things fare here. Ye must always feel free to contact us no matter where our trade takes us.”

Cyrus gave a deep nod. “Finish your raki. It is not a drink the women seem to care for. I have arranged a light repast this evening, with a grander welcome with close friends tomorrow.”

Pedr lifted his glass. “*Be salâmati.*” Tilting his head back, he downed the remainder of his drink.

Chapter Nineteen

Bayt al'asdiqa'
December 1301

Rona made her way down the staircase to Pedr's temporary office. Sunlight fell through the scalloped openings in the wall, painting the floor pale yellow. Her slippers whispered over the marble, the cool stone smooth beneath her feet. Mushegh padded alongside, his tail swaying gently over his back. Yasmina sprawled across the thick rug at Brant's feet, brilliant white against the warm red and gold threads.

Pedr glance up as she entered the room. His smile of welcome warmed her heart. Brant rose from his chair opposite Pedr's desk.

"*Sabah al-khayr*, Cousin" he said.

Rona laughed. "*Sabah an-noor*, Brant. Ye speak as though ye've lived here all yer life." She tousled his coppery blond hair. "Though ye dinnae look the part."

"I've learned quite a lot this trip," Brant said, clearly pleased with himself. "Haldor says I have a gift of languages . . .."

"He says ye talk a lot," Pedr corrected him with a laugh.

"Be that as it may, I've learned enough Farsi and Arabic to get me by, and enough Greek to order ouzo."

"The drink is *raki* while in Batroun," Pedr reminded him. "Dinnae ask for ouzo here."

"I dinnae like either," Rona said as she angled herself into a chair, feeling as awkward as a beached seal.

Pedr rounded the corner of the desk and helped her sit. "How do ye fare this morn?"

"I woke and ye were gone," she grumbled. A kiss to her temple mollified her somewhat, though the light stubble of his short beard rasped against her cheek as he touched hers lightly. As much as she liked the neatly-kept beard he'd grown since arriving in Batroun, today it sanded coarse against her skin. Not the first change she'd noted this day. She'd no appetite, either—an oddity after all she'd consumed growing this child inside her.

"I wished to let ye sleep. Ye tossed and turned quite a bit last night."

She shifted against the cushions, seeking a comfortable spot. "I thought I heard shouting a half-hour or so past. 'Tis what woke me."

Pedr frowned. "There was a wee disturbance beyond the gates. It appears to have subsided. Dinnae fash, *a leannan*. We are safe here."

She stiffened, her attention captured by noises outside the chamber.

"Nae. There it is, again."

Pedr straightened, head tilted toward the sounds. Angry shouts rose and fell amid the distinctive clatter of steel. Suddenly, a loud *boom* rocked the house, sending Yasmina bolting for safety beneath Pedr's desk. Mushegh whined and leaned against Rona's leg.

"What . . .?" Pedr shot a sharp look at Brant. Footsteps pounded in the passageway and Cyrus entered the chamber, his normal self-assured air unraveled, uncertainty slipping toward fear.

"There is a rabble in the street behind the house." He nodded to the far side of the room. "The walls should hold, but they've a device I've not seen before—only heard tales of."

"What is it?" Pedr demanded, his face dark with anger.

"A powder, something the Mongols brought with them from China. They guard the making of it well, but some say 'tis a mixture of sulphur, charcoal, and salt peter. When exposed to a flame, it will burn—very quickly and with much intensity."

"Like a flaming arrow?" Brant asked.

Cyrus shook his head. "This burns so swiftly as to cause what it touches to explode."

"That was the sound we heard? The boom?"

"Yes. The mixture can be placed inside an earthen container to which a thin rope is attached, lit, then tossed at the enemy—or over a wall. The shards of broken pottery are almost as injurious as the resulting flames of whatever catches fire."

Pedr turned to his cousin. "Brant, have the men who came here with ye from the *Dùdach Mara* patrol the yard. Watch for these . . .." He tilted his head to Cyrus.

"They are called *bombs*," the older man supplied.

"Watch for bombs. Have buckets readied to counter any flames."

"My men already patrol the yard," Cyrus said. "Have your soldiers report to Parun."

Brant gave a swift nod then hurried from the room. Pedr grabbed his belt and scabbard from the back of his chair and settled the leather about his hips, then checked the position of dirks at belt and boot.

Rona drew a breath, dread heavy in her chest. "Is the house under attack, or is this limited to the streets?"

"In the streets at this moment, my lady," Cyrus replied. "Howbeit, I have learned to take all such skirmishes seriously. Even if we are not directly involved, the rabble has no care for the innocents who may be harmed. The *zenana* is better protected than the rest of the house. Might I suggest ye return there until this is resolved?"

"Were I any more agile, I would decline yer suggestion—with all respect." Rona rubbed her mounded belly. "I will wait a bit longer, then do as ye suggest."

Cyrus inclined his head briskly then shifted his attention to Pedr. “We should hear news shortly.”

Another *boom* rattled the delicate tea set on the desk. Rona’s heart raced. Pedr settled his cloak about his shoulders.

“I will return anon, *mo chroi*. Stay here with Cyrus.”

“There is no need for ye to join the fray,” Cyrus said. “Should ye be needed, we will receive word.”

Both Rona and Pedr glanced at Cyrus as if he’d lost his mind.

“I dinnae ask my men to do what I willnae,” Pedr growled.

Cyrus raised a brow. “Patroling a yard, even one as vast as this one, does not require your skills, my friend. Your men will not think less of ye for biding here for a time. ’Tis not worth the risk of your child being born fatherless.”

Pedr’s jaw clenched and Rona knew Cyrus’s words had struck a chord. Pedr raised his eyes to hers, resolution on his face. A silent prayer slid through her. She would not ask him to stay with her to avoid injury. But Pedr was no longer the carefree, adventure-loving man she’d married. He was so much more. And he was about to become a father.

The skirmish outside the walls soon dissolved as the factions withdrew to fight another day. Rona played with Yasmina who had recovered from her earlier fear, keeping an ear for Pedr’s step in the passageway. She longed to be at his side, and found the wait intolerable, but she dared not risk harm to the babe.

I’m as likely to trip and fall as be injured by one of the rioters, I’m that clumsy. I’ve nae the balance or quickness of only a few weeks ago. She sighed and placed a hand over her belly, feeling a new ripple beneath her fingers that firmed her earlier suspicions.

We will have a new MacLean this day.

Relieved at Pedr's safe return only a short time later, Rona excused herself from the chamber when the contractions became too intense to cover their effect. Mushegh roused himself from his cushion and followed, but she shooed him back inside the room. Pedr glanced up, leaving Brant and Cyrus in the middle of their reports as he crossed the room to her side.

"Are ye well? Ye have been uncharacteristically quiet since I returned."

"I am well," she replied. "Ye should finish yer talk soon. I believe ye'll meet yer son this evening."

His eyes widened. He swept her into his arms, though he staggered a step with the extra burden. Long strides took him down the passageway and around the edge of the courtyard to the *zenana*.

Dhespina met them at the doorway.

"Please send for Sabi-Melek." Rona sent Dhespina a rueful look over Pedr's shoulder as he carried her to the bed in the center of the room. "I may have cut my timing a wee bit short."

"Ye should not have been involved in the riot," Dhespina scolded, first at Rona, then at Pedr.

"Och, my skills werenae needed, though I've fended off pirates before," Rona protested, "and the rabble outside yer gates . . .." She gasped as another contraction slid across her belly.

"Ye are a woman of peculiar talents—I've said so before," Dhespina replied, ignoring Pedr as she unbraided Rona's hair and helped her into a loose robe.

"Dinnae dither," Pedr rumbled. "My wife needs help."

"Ye are not needed here," Dhespina said, pointing to Pedr. "Ye will merely be in the way."

"Dinnae fash. All will be fine," Rona told him, smiling at his almost panicked look. He might be in his element facing a storm or pirates or a rabble in the streets, but this was new—and frightening—to them both.

He gently brushed the backs of his fingers across her cheek. "Ye have my heart, ye know."

"Aye. Now, let me get on with bringing this child into the world. He's a wee bit impatient."

After a long moment, Pedr gave a nod then left the chamber.

"We will keep the door closed to keep the *jinns* from entering. Soraya, see that every window and cabinet is unlatched to help ensure a safe delivery."

The maid bustled about the room as bid. Rona huffed through another pain. Dhespina brought her a chalice of wine and spices and bid her sip slowly.

"Dhespina." Soraya motioned to the door. "Sabi-Melek has arrived."

Rona glanced at the wizened midwife whom she'd met several weeks earlier. Another contraction swept through her, the intensity overwhelming. Rona panted then sighed as the pain faded.

"Ye are late." Rona regretted her words and tone of voice, but Sabi-Melek did not appear offended.

"The roads are perilous this day," the old woman replied. "I brought Yahya," she added, as if this explained her lengthy travel.

"Who is Yahya?" Rona eyed the broad-hipped woman who stared placidly back.

Sabi-Melek did not reply as she inspected Rona from head to toe. Dhespina took Rona's hand and Yahya perched a hip on the opposite side of the bed. Rona's heart doubled its beat. Did she truly trust the customs and practices of childbirth in this foreign place?

"What are ye doing?"

"Yahya has always had easy deliveries. She is here to assist ye any way she might."

Yahya nodded and placed her hand on Rona's back, encouraging her to lean forward as she rubbed firm but gentle circles. The massage felt good and Rona relaxed slightly as Yahya continued, her trust restored.

"I have arrived just in time," Sabi-Melek said. "I believe 'tis time to push."

Rona bore down, pushing to the chant of the midwife, waiting impatiently as Sabi-Melek checked the babe, groaning with the effort of pushing the bairn into the world.

At last she was rewarded with the wailing cry of her newborn. Sabi-Melek placed the red-faced infant on her belly. Rona could not check her tears.

"Ye have a strong son," the midwife said. "May God be praised."

Epilogue

Bayt al'asdiqa'
Late January 1302

Rain beat upon the roof of *Bayt al'asdiqa'* but Rona had ears only for her son. His gurgles and coos seemed a fascinating language she never tired of hearing. She grinned as his tiny fingers latched onto a strand of her hair.

"Ye have the grip of a warrior, my son."

Mushegh's tail thumped the floor.

"And ye are a worthy champion, my friend," she told the dog which refused to leave the bairn's side. Yasmina flew across the room to pounce on Mushegh's tail, rolled once, then bounded through the door and vanished into the passageway.

Dhespina strolled into the room, instructing Soraya to leave her tray on a low table. Steam wafted from the pot, promising to ward off the winter chill.

"Ye must swaddle him," Dhespina scolded. "The cloths will help his limbs grow straight." She crossed to Rona's side and gazed fondly at the bairn.

"He is swaddled as he needs," Rona replied, unwilling to keep him confined for long periods of time. "See how strong he is?" She winced as the bairn gave a vigorous tug then gently removed her hair from his fingers.

"Do not say such things," Dhespina whispered. "Ye tempt the child stealers. He has yet to reach his fortieth day and must be protected. *The grave of a woman in accouchement and her child is open for forty days*," she quoted.

Rona glanced at the necklace of tiny blue beads Dhespina had presented the babe the day he was born. Said to protect against the evil eye, she'd also given one of blue jaspe to Rona. She fingered the smooth stones around her neck.

Protect this child.

She inspected him once more, ensuring his skin was clean and dry, then deftly wrapped him in soft wool swaddling. Cradling him in her arms, she rocked him gently as she sang a soft lullaby.

Hush-a-by, birdie, croon, croon
Hush-a-by, birdie, croon;
The sheep are gane tae the silver wood,
An the coos are gane tae the broom, broom.

An it's braw milkin the cattle, cattle,
It's braw milkin the cattle;
The birds are singin, the bells are ringin,
An the wild deer come gallopin by.

Hush-a-by birdie, croon, croon,
Hush-a-by birdie, croon,
The goats are gane tae the mountain hie,
An they'll no be hame till noon.

He resisted a few minutes before his eyelids closed but was soon fast asleep.

Dhespina motioned to the small pot. "Drink your tea before it cools. I will return anon."

Rona savored the warm drink, then, with a slow, swaying step, followed the passageway to Pedr's office.

Pedr glanced up as Rona appeared in the doorway, a grin breaking across his face at the sight of the bairn in Rona's arms.

"How does Wynn fare?"

Rona kissed Pedr's cheek. "He is well. Perfect, in fact. I

love that he bears yer ma's name."

"Aye. Ma will be pleased. She should hear of him soon and wish we were home so she could spoil him."

"Mayhap Alex and Peigi will present her with grandchildren soon. It may be some time before we are back in Scotland."

"I've wanted to speak to ye of this."

Rona placed the infant in the crook of Pedr's arm, warming to the sight. "He will sleep for a time. What do ye wish to discuss?"

"I'm nae agreeable to remaining here much longer. The instability worries me, and I believe 'tis time to consider returning home."

Rona pondered this for a moment. "I havenae heard a repeat of the *stramash* last month, though I dinnae step beyond these walls. I am ready to travel again, despite the forty day restriction set upon women who have just given birth, but I had imagined we would continue to sail the trade routes for a time."

"I understand, *mo chroi*, and I had thought to trade amongst the Greek Isles, mayhap even beyond Constantinople to ports in the Black Sea."

Pedr ran a fingertip over his son's tiny nose and across one plump, pink cheek then glanced at Rona. "But I must consider ye and Wynn. My priorities have shifted. Having ye with me is verra important, and I willnae ask ye to remain behind when I sail, yet I must find ways to protect ye."

Rona gave a slow nod. "I'm anxious to have the boards and sea beneath my feet once again. Howbeit, I had not given thought to the political unrest in the area—nor how widespread 'tis."

She fingered the fine wool wrapped about her son's tiny body, a surge of protectiveness unlike any she'd experienced earlier causing tears to rise. "I would give my life for his. Yet, I would prefer to live long enough to give him brothers and sisters, and to hold our grandchildren."

Pedr pulled her hard against him, his face buried in her hair. His breath slid warm against her ear.

"There are nae trade goods in this port nor any other worth risking yer life, *a leannan*."

"What news do Haldor and Brant bring?"

"Crippling taxes, outbursts of clashes between the remaining Latins, Turkish ghazis, Mongols, and Mamluks. Disruptions in harvest, and likely in the planting season ahead from the rebellions. The Silk Road remains open, though caravans must spend much gold to hire mercenaries for protection—and hope no one pays them more to betray them."

"The risk is enormous." Rona sighed. "Nae guarantee what we will find at a port, even if the trade is confirmed ahead of time."

"'Tis my fear, also. Do ye agree 'tis time to go home?"

She nodded. "Aye, husband. 'Tis time."

Pedr kissed her cheek. "As soon as 'tis safe for ye and Wynn to travel, we'll make plans. I think it best we dinnae linger over-long."

"Dhespina and Sabi-Melek insist we confine ourselves to the *zenana* for at least another sennight, though I've nae seen a woman lie idle so long who wasnae perilously ill. 'Tis been just over a month since Wynn's birth, and he and I are verra well."

"Then we will begin arranging the loading of the *Dùdach Mara.* Mayhap we will lift anchor within a fortnight's time. Some things will of necessity be loaded aboard the next ship. Fruits and vegetables arenae ready, though we will take some for our personal use from the protected gardens here." He touched his forehead to hers. "Do what ye must to prepare."

"I will be glad to have ye to myself again," she whispered, yearning to have his arms about her, to return to the intimacies they shared before Wynn had been born. She knew the reasons Sabi-Melek cautioned her against leaving the *zenana* or making love with her husband until the proscribed time had passed, but the midwife's advice chafed against her need.

Pedr chuckled. "There will be plenty to distract us aboard ship, even without our bairn."

"I wish . . .."

"What do ye wish, *mo chroí*?"

"I want to be in yer arms, though . . .."

"Dinnae rush things. I am content to hold ye and Wynn and count my many blessings."

Rona's chest tightened, first with tears, then with a sense of euphoria. Fatigue quickly followed. Would her tumultuous feelings ever return to normal?

A tap at the door interrupted them. Cyrus stood in the portal, a troubled look on his face. Pedr ushered him inside with a wave of his hand.

"Please, have a seat."

"I fear I bring bad news."

Pedr handed Wynn to Rona then took the missive from Cyrus's hand and unrolled the small packet. He perused the contents, translating the Greek script as he read.

To my friend Cyrus,

Praying this finds ye safe and well, and your family under God's blessing.

I find myself in a tenuous position and must beg a tremendous favor, the granting of which may put ye in danger.

The situation in Constantinople is such that it has become imperative my daughter and I leave the city at once. Since my wife's passing, relations have been strained between her family and myself, and we can no longer claim their protection. As difficulties continue to escalate between Rome and Constantinople, I find my neighbors increasingly hostile twoard those who follow the Roman Church, and movement about the city is fraught with danger which grows daily.

Two days ago, another family in my situation was attacked in their home, the mother and father left for dead, and their three daughters abducted—one can only guess their fate as the slave markets thrive.

Cyrus, I fear I will not make it out of Constantinople and must make a difficult decision. I have charged my personal guard, a man of great honesty and loyalty, to spirit my daughter, Aelia, from the city this very night whilst I remain behind to deflect suspicion. He is to travel to Smyrna and await further orders there. Smyrna is a well-known port, one ye can perhaps reach with only minimal effort and within a sennight's travel if all goes well.

To off-set your costs, I have enclosed gold coins and a necklace which once belonged to my wife—all I can lay my hands on at this time. If there is a MacLean ship in the area, or one scheduled to arrive soon, I beg ye book passage for Aelia to England where she might find refuge with my family in Maldon. Do not trouble about me. I will make my own fate in the coming days. I will do so with peace knowing my daughter has your help.

The MacLeans will not refuse my plea. They claim a debt owed for my grandfather's swift actions on Donal's behalf more than fifty years ago, and though I would not ask it for myself, I would barter for my daughter's life.

Be safe, my friend.

If I make it to Batroun, I will owe ye more than I can ever repay.

Mihal Maldes

Pedr read the missive once again in silence as his sense

of honor warred with the import of what might lay ahead.

Rona touched his hand, her fingers warm against his skin. "We cannae allow his daughter to come to harm. I can have our things readied within a few days—less if need be."

"I could go alone."

"Nae. I willnae be parted from ye. Neither in this life nor the next."

He shook his head. "This could be a simple thing, or it could be a battle for our lives."

Rona smiled. "Then 'twill be a good thing to have a pirate on board, aye?"

Port of Batroun
Early February, 1302

Brant and Haldor met them at the dock, grins wide as they greeted Rona and their new nephew. Wynn's eyes widened at the loud snap of the sails, his mouth rounded with surprise at the sound. He kicked his legs inside his heavy blanket and chortled.

"He's a true MacLean," Haldor approved. "He will take to the sea like a bird to the sky."

Rona beamed at the warm welcome. Though their immediate future appeared fraught with peril, she could not imagine living without the sway of the sea beneath her feet nor the absence of her MacLean family. No matter where the wind blew, aboard the *Dùdach Mara* was where she belonged.

Rona drew a deep breath, inhaling the cold salt air. The cry of birds and shouts of sailors aboard neighboring ships filled her ears, chasing away her fears and filling her with excitement.

It was good to be home.

"Permission to come aboard?" she asked. Murdo raced

across the deck, barking his greeting, stubby tail wagging fiercely. He leapt easily from the deck onto the dock, nose to the planks as he circled Rona's feet. With a yip of recognition, he sat, staring up at Rona while his entire rump wiggled excitedly.

Haldor inclined his head. "Permission granted."

~The End~

Follow Rona and Pedr and discover what awaits in *The Highlander's Byzantine Bride,* available fall 2021. Check out the rest of the Hardy Heroines series for more action-packed romance with strong heroines and deeply-researched historical story lines on Amazon

If you enjoyed Rona's and Pedr's story in The Highlander's Pirate Bride, please consider leaving a review.

For fun information about the ideas behind this book (we love research!) keep reading!

Author's Notes

We had so much fun writing this book. It was originally written for a holiday box set entitled Merry Mayhem: A Yuletide Collection of Rogues and Outlaws, a premise we couldn't resist.

As always, the early 1300s were full of fascinating plots and counter-plots. Here is some of the history behind Pedr's and Rona's story.

First of all, **Pedr and Alex** were introduced in The Highlander's Welsh Bride. You can read Birk's and Carys's story in The Highlander's Welsh Bride. If you'd like to read more tales of smart, courageous women, you'll find Hanna's and Arbela's stories in The Highlander's Norse Bride and The Highlander's Crusader Bride, and in the rest of the Hardy Heroines series.

Nyvaig ship. The Hebridean galley (aka birlinn) was a great coastal trading ship, but often fell prey to Viking longships. The nyvaig ship was a new design by Somerled (King of the Isles), incorporating innovations such as a hinged rudder to make the birlinn capable of outmaneuvering the Norse longships in close quarters. The new design can be seen on Somerled's seal here: http://clandonald-heritage.com/the-rising-eagle/ under the heading "Seal of the Lords of the Isles"

Murdo, whose name means *sea warrior*, was a terrier of a breed which would eventually become the West Highland White Terrier. The Westie, as it's affectionately known, originated hundreds of years ago in Argyllshire, and came in a variety of colors, for only the best hunters, regardless of color, were considered for breeding. Then, in the 19th century, Colonel Edward Donald Malcolm, 16th Laird of Poltalloch, lost his best terrier in a hunting accident when the red-coated dog was mistaken for a fox. He resolved to never have that happen again and began breeding only white or cream-colored dogs which came to be known as the Poltalloch Terrier. The modern West Highland White Terrier is a combination of the Poltalloch Terrier, the Pittenweem Terrier, and the Roseneath Terrier.

Mushegh is a Gampr, an ancient breed of dog known primarily as a herding or livestock protection dog—much like a Great Pyrenese which you may be familiar with. Gampr means 'big hairy beast', and they were also known as 'Gelkheght' which means 'wolf-choker'. They are a little shorter than a German Shepherd with a short, dense coat which protects them from both harsh, cold winters and hot, dry summers, and a long tail which curls at the end.

Cyrus's cats are Angoras, with roots deep into the past. They are incredibly social, get along well with other cats as well as dogs, and bond with their human family as well. Angoras are also known for their playfulness and are one of the few domestic cat breeds who enjoy swimming. Deafness does run in the Turkish Angora cat and seems to be linked to the blue eye color and white hair coat.

Raki is a distilled drink made from the by-products of grapes (usually skins and stems) which have been previously used to make wine, and flavored with anise.

Bombs and gunpowder were invented by the Chinese and used against Mongol invaders as early as 904 A.D. "Flying fire", a tube of gunpowder attached to an arrow—

looking much like bottle rockets you may shoot on holidays—early forms of hand grenades, incendiaries, land mines, and other weapons packed quite a surprise against the invaders. By the 1200s, the Chinese were filling clay pots—or bombs—with gunpowder and firing them from catapults. The Mongols spread this knowledge west as they conquered lands from Asia to the Middle East. Despite the efforts to keep the ingredients of gunpowder secret, by 1280 recipes had been published in the west, and we find mention of a children's toy resembling a very small firecracker in 1267, and drawings of a European cannon by Walter de Milemete in 1326. These weapons sported colorful—and often intimidating—descriptions as fire lances, 'magic fire meteor going against the wind', and 'thunder crash bomb'.

Aonghus Og MacDonnell. We could write an entire story of the rise of the MacDonald clan and the Lords of the Isles. The link which fascinated us the most led us to Finlaggan and the very heart of the MacDonalds. You can read more about it here if you wish: https://www.islayinfo.com/finlaggan_clan_donald.html

MacLean Shipping and the Levant. The original MacLean story (The Highlander's Crusader Bride) set up the series for a family with roots in Scotland and ties to the Holy Land. However, by 1300, the Crusader State of Tripoli had fallen, first to the Mongols, then to the Mamluks. Shia Muslims and the Druze were in rebellion against the Mamluks who were busy fighting European Crusaders attempting to retake Acre, and Mongols invading their northern and eastern borders. With the loss of nearly everything Donal MacLean would have left behind when he returned to Scotland, we decided the MacLean barony in Batroun (a fictional title) would have disappeared about the time Tripoli was lost to the Mongols.

Acknowledgements

We are happy to have Lane McFarland and Cate Parke with us again as critique partners and beta readers for this story. There's no possible way to write these tales without them.

And a huge shout out to our cover artist, Dar Albert, who took our thoughts, said she 'had an idea', and came up with a fantastic cover! I don't think we changed a thing!

Author Bios

Cathy MacRae lives behind the cheese curtain where she and her husband read, write, and tend the garden—with the help of the dogs, of course.

You can visit with her on Facebook or read her blogs and learn about her books at www.cathymacraeauthor.com. Drop her a line—she loves to hear from readers!

To keep up with new releases and other fun things, sign up for her newsletter! (You'll find DD's news there, too!)

Other ways to connect with Cathy:
Facebook
Twitter: @CMacRaeAuthor
Instagram: cathymacrae_author
Pinterest
Book bub

DD MacRae enjoys bringing history to life and considers research one of the best things about writing a story! With more than 35 years of martial arts training, DD also brings breath-taking action to the tales.

You can connect with DD through www.cathymacraeauthor.com. It's always exciting to hear from readers!

More Books by Cathy & DD MacRae

The Hardy Heroine series

Highland Escape **(book 1)**
The Highlander's Viking Bride **(book 2)**
The Highlander's Crusader Bride **(book 3)**
The Highlander's Norse Bride, a Novella **(book 4)**
The Highlander's Welsh Bride **(book 5)**
The Prince's Highland Bride **(book 6)**
The Highlander's Pirate Bride **(book 7)**

by DD MacRae
The Italian Billionaire's Runaway Bride

By Cathy MacRae

The Highlander's Bride series

The Highlander's Accidental Bride **(book 1)**
The Highlander's Reluctant Bride **(book 2)**
The Highlander's Tempestuous Bride **(book 3)**
The Highlander's Outlaw Bride **(book 4)**
The Highlander's French Bride **(book 5)**

Christmas novellas

Mhàiri's Yuletide Wish

Brenna's Yuletide Song

Novellas on the Scottish Border
The Saint
The Penitent
The Cursed

The Ghosts of Culloden Moor series
(with LL Muir, Diane Darcy, Jo Jones, and Melissa Mayhue)

Adam
Malcolm
MacLeod
Patrick

License Notes

www.ingramcontent.com/pod-product-compliance
Lightning Source LLC
LaVergne TN
LVHW010619100826
845148LV00014B/3031

9781736685204